D0827718

FROM THE
NANCY DREW FILES

THE CASE: Nancy investigates the identity of Natalia Petronov's father . . . and of the person threatening to kill her!

CONTACT: Natalia's partner and boyfriend, trapeze artist Hayden Gentry requests Nancy's assistance.

SUSPECTS: Katrina Van Swalla—the third member of the circus trapeze act, she'd like to swing with Hayden . . . without Natalia getting in the way.

Marshall Keiser—the owner of the circus, he's heard that Natalia wants to jump to a rival . . . and he's mad enough to feed someone to the lions.

The Pomatto Brothers—a couple of circus daredevils, they may be the only ones capable of driving the motorcycle that nearly ran Natalia down.

COMPLICATIONS: Only one person knows the whole truth about Natalia's past and her real father: her adoptive mother Vera Petronov. But she's determined to keep the secret . . . forever.

Books in The Nancy Drew Files® Series

Available from ARCHWAY Paperbacks

The Nancy Drew Files™

Case 82
Dangerous Relations
Carolyn Keene

AN ARCHWAY PAPERBACK
Published by POCKET BOOKS
New York London Toronto Sydney Tokyo Singapore

AN ARCHWAY PAPERBACK *Original*

An Archway Paperback published by
POCKET BOOKS, a division of Simon & Schuster Inc.
1230 Avenue of the Americas, New York, NY 10020

Copyright © 1993 by Simon & Schuster Inc.
Produced by Mega-Books of New York, Inc.

ISBN: 0-671-73086-X

First Archway Paperback printing April 1993

10 9 8 7 6 5 4 3 2 1

NANCY DREW, AN ARCHWAY PAPERBACK and colophon are registered trademarks of Simon & Schuster Inc.

THE NANCY DREW FILES is a trademark of Simon & Schuster Inc.

Cover art by Tricia Zimic

Printed in the U.S.A.

IL 6+

Chapter

One

"Aᴜᴛʜᴏʀɪᴢᴇᴅ ᴠᴇʜɪᴄʟᴇs ᴏɴʟʏ." Nancy Drew read aloud the sign on the gate just outside the Grand Royal Circus. She nosed the car she had rented at the Sarasota Airport into a space in the shade of a palm tree.

Bess Marvin, Nancy's good friend, yawned and fluffed her long blond hair. "How'd you ever talk me into a middle of the night flight?"

"I promised you sunny Florida, that's how," Nancy reminded her, climbing out of the car.

"It sure feels warm compared to the weather we left in River Heights," George Fayne said. George was Bess's cousin, and the three girls were almost inseparable.

"Humid, too. Your hair is curling." Bess gave her cousin's short dark curls a little pat. Then she

1

shivered. "But is it warm enough to go to the beach?"

"Don't even think about it," Nancy said in a mock-stern tone. "We're here to work, remember?"

Though she was only eighteen, Nancy had quite a reputation as a detective. She had been intrigued when Hayden Gentry, trainer and catcher for a flying trapeze act, had called her a week earlier and asked for her help. His girlfriend, Natalia Petronov, wanted to find her biological father.

Natalia had been born in Moscow, so the chances that an American detective could find Natalia's father were slim, but Hayden seemed to think Nancy might be able to do it. And Nancy was willing to try—especially since it meant spending a few days with the circus in Florida!

Nancy stopped inside the gate and took a long look at the circus grounds. It was a rectangular lot, longer than a football field. Parking for the twenty or thirty travel trailers began at her right, then turned and followed the fence along the width of the field. There were buildings, stock pens, and an outdoor ring on the opposite side of the lot. Around the entire perimeter of the grounds was a beaten track. In the middle of the lot, men and machines were working to raise a huge red-and-white canvas tent.

Hammers rang out as workers made repairs on bleachers. Other workers were painting a concession wagon, a ticket box, and souvenir stands. The scents of dust and paint hung in the morning air.

"Look at the elephant!" Bess exclaimed, pointing to the huge beast harnessed to a cable.

"Bet he's going to raise the tent," George said, edging closer.

As the girls watched, a bearded man with a cigar clamped in one corner of his mouth left the workers and hurried over to them. "Can I help you?" he asked.

"We're looking for Hayden Gentry," Nancy said, then introduced herself.

"Oh—the detective," the man said in a neutral tone. "I'm Marshall Keiser. I own this mud show."

"Hayden said you're going on the road in less than a week. Looks like a big job, getting everything ready," Nancy said.

"Yep," Keiser said. "Rehearsals start tomorrow, and things are hectic." He shouted to the elephant trainer, "Okay, Burton. Bring it up now."

The elephant pulled hard on the cable. The flag at the top of the pole flapped as it slowly and steadily, rose to vertical position.

"Whoa!"

As Keiser motioned to the trainer, Nancy noticed a tattoo on his muscled arm. It was of a motorcycle and had Born to Get Even written below it. Turning back to her, Keiser said,

"Hayden and Natalia will be practicing—assuming Her Excellency isn't too big-headed to practice."

"'Her Excellency'?" Nancy echoed.

But Keiser didn't explain his sarcasm. Instead, he pointed across the grassy lot to the buildings. "The tall one's the practice arena."

Nancy thanked him, then started across the lot with Bess and George at her side.

"Hey!" Keiser shouted. "Go back to the road and follow it around. Can't have you in the way with the tent going up."

Wondering if he was always so abrupt, Nancy led her friends back to the path. And what had he meant by calling Natalia Her Excellency?

"What's a mud show?" George asked.

"A tent circus. A little rain, and the lot turns to mud," Nancy explained as they walked past the row of trailers. "This is the winter home for the circus. They're getting ready to take it on the road."

Nancy looked with interest at a large mesh globe that sat between two trailers. The steel ball was so big that a small car would have fit snugly inside.

"That's a prop for a motorcycle stunt," George told her and Bess. "The rider rides his bike inside the globe. I've seen it on TV."

Nancy smelled the aroma of coffee as they passed another trailer. She wondered if it was the circus's cookhouse. Next to it was a circus ring

4

where a woman was working some beautiful dappled horses.

Finally they reached the corrugated steel arena. Inside, colorful circus posters hung along a wide hallway. Nancy noticed an office door with Marshall Keiser's nameplate on it and a second door labeled Props.

At the end of the hallway was a large open room that served as the practice area. Mats and riggings were everywhere. Nancy saw a red-haired woman mount a trampoline near the center of the room. Not far from her, a man and woman were stretching on mats. The man had a muscular build, blond hair, and bright blue eyes.

"Is that Hayden?" Bess asked.

"I think so," Nancy said. "I only met him once, two years ago when he was visiting River Heights. His aunt is a friend of Hannah."

Hannah Gruen, the housekeeper for Nancy and her father, had invited Hayden and his aunt over for dinner. Hayden, twenty-four at the time, had seemed a lot older than Nancy. Of course, she'd still been in high school then.

Hayden's face lit up with a smile as he spotted Nancy coming. He got up from the mat, went over to her, and shook her hand warmly. "It's great to see you again, Nancy. I'd like you to meet Natalia Petronov."

Natalia, who had followed him over to the spot where the group was standing, had brown hair neatly coiled on the back of her head. She had deep-set dark eyes, high cheekbones, a firm chin, and a sweet smile. Nancy liked her instantly.

Nancy introduced Bess and George. Natalia greeted the three girls enthusiastically. "Hayden's aunt is always sending him clippings about the cases you've solved," she told Nancy. "I can't thank you enough for coming."

Nancy smiled. "I just hope I can help you."

"Are you the only ones practicing?" George asked, looking around.

Natalia nodded. "Nine o'clock is our time to use the gym."

"The high-wire team, which usually practices after us, is helping set up the big top today, so we'll get a little extra time," Hayden said.

"And we can sure use it," Natalia said. "We do two local shows before we go on the road, and we're still smoothing out the edges."

The red-haired woman leapt off the trampoline and came over. Nancy guessed she was in her mid- to late twenties. Hayden introduced her as Katrina Van Swalla, the third and last member of the aerial team.

Katrina greeted them, then turned away, saying, "Can we get started?"

As Nancy looked on, Katrina climbed a rope ladder to a small platform high above the ring. The bar, which hung from rope cables, squeaked as she caught it with a hook and pulled it toward her. Nancy watched a moment, thinking Katrina was going to swing out on it. But she simply stood on the platform, holding it. Perhaps she was preparing herself mentally.

"I didn't realize you'd get here this early," Hayden apologized.

"Oh, go ahead and practice. We'd love to watch," Nancy said. Bess and George echoed agreement.

"When you see the girls fly, you'll understand why we call our act Angel Wings," Hayden said proudly.

"Hayden's such a great catcher, he makes us look good." Natalia smiled at him and started up the same ladder Katrina had just climbed.

Hayden scaled a second ladder and stood alone on a platform that faced the one on which Natalia and Katrina waited. A trapeze bar hung near each platform. One was for the catcher, the other for the leaper. The object, Nancy knew, was for the leaper to let go of the bar, fly through the air, be caught by the catcher, then return to the other bar.

"There are some chairs against the wall," Nancy said. "Let's go sit down."

"Katrina's got an eye for fashion," said Bess, who loved clothes. "I like the way her pink sash dresses up that leotard," she went on as she sat down.

George, who was a natural athlete and cared little about fashion, said, "Trapeze artists have to be great athletes. Strength and timing are all-important." She sat down beside Nancy, and they all looked up expectantly at the trapeze artists.

Nancy's breath caught as Hayden swung onto his bar. He built speed, then brought his legs straight up. The muscles in his calves stood out as he wrapped his legs around the heavy ropes from which the bar was extended.

"That guy's really strong," George murmured as Hayden released his hands and hung upside down. He kept swinging at a steady pace.

"Warm up with a backward somersault. You first, Natalia," Hayden called.

Natalia swung out on the bar. "She must be thirty feet off the ground!" Nancy exclaimed.

"I'd be scared to death," Bess said, her blue eyes wide. "Even *with* a safety net!"

Natalia brought her feet between her hands on the bar. With lightning-quick grace, the young flyer did a back somersault off the bar. Time stood still as she sailed through the air. Then came a slapping sound. Natalia and Hayden locked hands around wrists. The catch was made! It was so quiet in the arena, Nancy heard Hayden's *whoof* of exertion on the backswing.

"Wow!" George breathed, her dark eyes aglow.

But the trick wasn't over. In the next heartbeat, Hayden released Natalia. Nancy saw Natalia's mask of concentration as she twisted and sailed back toward her own bar. The young flyer stretched out, reaching. Then her fingers touched the bar. She'd caught it! Nancy thought.

She opened her mouth to cheer, when Natalia's hands slipped. Nancy could only watch in horror as Natalia plunged down, her body twisting out of control.

Chapter

Two

NATALIA CRASHED into the safety net and bounced up again. Nancy dashed over. "Are you hurt?" she called. "Should we get a doctor?"

"Lie still, Nat. I'm coming!" Hayden cried, scrambling down the ladder.

"I'm okay," Natalia said in a shaky voice. She grabbed the edge of the net and rolled out.

"What happened?" Hayden asked, steadying her.

Natalia's hand trembled as she reached for a towel. "The bar was slippery."

"Slippery?" Nancy echoed.

From the platform, Katrina called down, "If the show's over, could we get back to work?"

Nancy saw Natalia stiffen as she retorted, "I didn't fall on purpose, Katrina!"

10

"What was it then—clumsiness?" the redhead taunted, startling Nancy with her meanness.

Natalia tossed the towel down. "There was something slick on the bar. My hands slipped."

"Oh, please!"

Nancy heard controlled anger in Hayden's voice as he said, "Katrina, let's take a break."

Katrina made a graceful free-fall into the net. "See, Natalia? That's the way it's *supposed* to be done."

Trying to ignore Katrina's rudeness, Nancy looked up. "Are the trapezes fastened to the rigging with something oily?"

Hayden pointed to what looked like a steel pipe. "Two collars are bolted to that crane bar. Rigging hooks connect the ropes to the collars."

"Could oil have dripped from the connections?" Nancy asked.

"It was carelessness," Katrina cut in.

"Or somebody oiled the bar!" Natalia retorted.

Nancy looked at her in alarm. Did she really believe that? And why was she breathing so hard?

Hayden noticed, too. "You don't sound so good, Nat."

"Oh, great! Now she's going to have an asthma attack!" Katrina rolled her green eyes. "Well, call me when it's over. I'm going to the cookhouse for coffee."

Stunned by her behavior, Nancy watched the

redhead walk away. She disappeared out into the hallway.

"Stress sometimes causes these attacks," Hayden explained, as he reached for Natalia's large canvas tote bag. "Nat, your inhaler's empty."

"I'll have to go back to my trailer," Natalia said in a choked voice. "I have another one there."

She sounded to Nancy like someone who'd run a long, hard race and was trying to catch her breath. Alarmed, she asked, "Is there anything we can do?"

"I'm so so-sorry. You—came—all this way." Natalia tried to apologize between gasps.

"You can't help it," Nancy said, following them to the hallway. "We can talk when you're feeling better."

"Can you come by Nat's trailer in an hour or so?" Hayden asked as they started down the hallway. "It's the pink one straight across the lot. There's a big steel globe parked between it and the next trailer—you can't miss it."

"I know where you mean," Nancy said.

"I sure wouldn't want to work with someone who hated me like that," Bess said when they were alone in the corridor.

"Me, either." George's gaze was troubled. "In trapeze work, your life is in your teammates' hands. That sort of tension is dangerous."

12

Nancy was disturbed, too. Especially considering Natalia's comment about someone oiling the bar. Frowning, she said, "Let's check that towel Natalia wiped her hands on."

At first glance the towel looked snowy white. But as Nancy turned it over, she spotted a dull, nearly colorless smudge.

"She got something on her hands, all right," Nancy said. She held the towel up to her nose, but all she could smell was fabric softener. She folded the towel, put it into her shoulder bag, then looked up at the trapeze riggings, remembering Katrina holding the bar while Natalia was climbing up. Had she put something on it? "I'm going to climb up and check that bar."

"Be careful!" Bess cautioned.

Nancy hoisted herself up to the first rung of the rope ladder. It creaked and swayed beneath her weight, but she held on and kept climbing until she reached the platform.

The trapeze, hanging down from the ceiling, was just out of reach. But fastened to one rail of the platform was a rod with a hook on the end of it. As Katrina had done, Nancy used it to pull the trapeze toward her. She took a tissue from the pocket of her jeans and started wiping the bar. There was nothing on the edges, but when she wiped near the center, she found oily smudges.

"Here, George. Catch." Nancy let the tissue drift down. She descended the ladder.

THE NANCY DREW FILES

"Do you think it's oil off the rigging?" George asked, passing the tissue back to Nancy once she was on the ground.

"I can't tell," Nancy said. She put the tissue in her shoulder bag next to the towel. Her father had a friend on the Sarasota police force, Phillip Green. Maybe he would ask the police crime lab to analyze the smudges for her.

"Do you think someone oiled the bar on purpose?" Bess asked.

That was precisely what Nancy was wondering. Katrina? Or someone else? And why? Could the accident in any way be linked to Natalia's plan to search for her father?

There was only one place to start. "Let's find Katrina," Nancy said.

Just outside the arena, two dark-haired young men were polishing the chrome on their motorcycles.

"Excuse me," Bess said. "We're looking for someone."

The taller of the two eyed her with a bold smile. "I hope it's me."

Bess smiled. "I'm Bess Marvin. These are my friends George Fayne and Nancy Drew."

"So you're the detective. We heard you were coming," the boy said to Nancy.

"You did? Who told you?" Nancy asked.

"Natalia. She's pretty excited about looking for her dad." He grinned and extended his hand.

"I'm Eduardo Pomatto. This is my brother Joseph."

"Hello," Joseph said shyly.

"Nice to meet you," Nancy said. She looked around. "Could you tell us where the cookhouse is?"

"We'll show you," Eduardo offered. He dropped his polishing rag and wiped off his hands.

"Are you performers?" Bess asked.

Eduardo nodded. "We do a motorcycle act called Sphere of Death. Heard of it?"

Remembering the steel globe, Nancy exclaimed, "That big mesh globe! You ride inside it?"

Joseph smiled. "That's right."

George said, "One time on a stunt show, I saw a couple of brothers riding motorcycles inside a round cage like that. Their mother was inside it, too. They rode loops around her—upside down and everything. It was wild!"

"Was it you two?" Bess asked, her eyes wide.

Eduardo shook his head. "No way. Our mother is too smart for that!"

Everyone laughed. Still chatting, Eduardo led them into the eatery they'd passed earlier. Nancy glanced down the tables that lined two walls. The place was crowded, but she didn't see Katrina.

The girls poured themselves glasses of juice at the buffet, then followed Joseph and Eduardo to a long table at which six men were sitting. Eduardo introduced the girls to the men. "These guys are clowns. That's Slowpoke there at the end. The skinny one beside him is Jiffy. This is Dillard and Winky and Packrat and Tim."

Tim had pale blond hair. He reached across the table and bowed over each of the girls' hands. But instead of releasing Nancy's hand, he brought it to his lips and kissed it, then pretended his lips were stuck.

"Tim had peanut butter for breakfast," Slowpoke said.

"Oldest trick in the book," Jiffy muttered.

Nancy, Bess, and George joined in the laughter. Several of the clowns jumped up and went to get folding chairs for the girls. Then everyone moved, to make room for them and the Pomatto brothers. Just as everyone settled into their chairs, Packrat poked Tim and said in a stage whisper, "Here comes Red."

The blond clown's face lit up. He waved and called, "There's room over here, Katrina."

Nancy was pleased when Katrina brought over a chair and a cup of tea and squeezed in between Tim and Packrat. Anxious to see what she could learn, Nancy smiled across the table and said, "I was sorry practice ended so abruptly. I was looking forward to seeing you perform."

"Oh?" Katrina said guardedly, then took a sip of her tea.

Nancy nodded. "It must take a lot of hard work to be a good flyer. How'd you get started?"

When Katrina seemed reluctant to answer, Tim said, "Kat was a great platform diver in high school. Go on, tell her, Katrina."

Nancy could see by the look in his eye that Tim had a crush on Katrina. "You two knew each other in high school?"

Tim nodded. "We both grew up in Sarasota. It's a circus town. It's easy to get bitten by the circus bug."

Now Katrina was looking less sullen. Apparently, she enjoyed Tim's attention.

Bess asked her, "How'd you go from diving to flying?"

"The circus bug, as Tim said," Katrina replied. "I asked a retired trapeze artist to give me lessons. Tim and I joined different circuses, but we've both been with the Grand Royal for about three years now."

"Isn't it scary to fall? What causes that, anyway?" Nancy asked innocently.

"Mostly, it's a poorly timed trick," Katrina said. "Hayden decides whether or not to catch a trick. If it isn't coming at him right, he'll let it go rather than risk not being able to hang on to it throughout the swing."

"So even pros fall?" Nancy asked.

"Oh, sure," Katrina said. "Though during shows, Hayden sometimes catches tricks he ought to let pass. Especially Natalia's. Guess he wants to make her look good," she added.

Noticing that Tim's attention had strayed to his friends, Nancy reached into her bag and pulled out the towel Natalia had wiped her hands on.

"Natalia was telling the truth about the bar being oily. Look at this," Nancy said, waiting for Katrina's reaction.

"Looks like Natalia had something on her hands when she left the platform," Katrina said in a sharp voice.

"I don't think she'd be that careless," Nancy said. Watching Katrina carefully, she added, "Natalia thought you had something to do with it."

The redhead jumped to her feet, nearly spilling her tea. "You've got no right to accuse me! Take that back or you'll be sorry!"

The chatter at the table stopped dead. Nancy felt every face in the room turn her way. Tim the clown leapt out of his chair as Katrina stormed around the table and came straight at Nancy!

Chapter

Three

ALARMED, Nancy pushed her chair back and stood to defend herself. But Joseph Pomatto jumped up, too, and stepped in front of Nancy.

"Whoa, whoa, calm down, Katrina," he said soothingly.

"Kat, take it easy." Tim slipped his arm through Katrina's. "Come on, let's take a little walk." He cast a glance at Nancy. "Don't mind Kat. She didn't mean anything. It's just been pretty tense around here lately, with the show coming up."

"Of course," Nancy said, though she didn't think much of Tim's excuse.

Katrina glowered at Nancy, then turned and stormed out of the cookhouse. Tim followed at her heels, and the door banged shut after them.

Eduardo blew out his breath. "What did you say to make Katrina so mad?" he asked.

Briefly Nancy described what had happened during practice. All the clowns listened in. Finishing, she said, "Maybe someone oiled the bar as a prank. Or do you think it was meant to do serious harm?"

When the men seemed reluctant to speak up, George said, "Well, I don't know much about trapeze artists, but it seems to me that either way, Natalia could have gotten hurt."

"You're right," Jiffy said. "A flyer needs to hit the net in a horizontal position. Otherwise, he or she could bounce right off it."

"That's what causes injuries," Packrat added. "A few flyers have died that way." Packrat drained his coffee cup and rose to go. The other clowns said goodbye, then followed him out.

The clowns hadn't answered her, Nancy mused. Hoping to do better with the Pomatto brothers, she asked, "Would Katrina purposely hurt Natalia?"

Eduardo frowned. "Well, Katrina didn't exactly like getting her boyfriend stolen," he said slowly.

"Natalia stole Katrina's boyfriend?" Nancy repeated, startled. "You mean Hayden?"

Eduardo nodded. "Hayden and Katrina came to Grand Royal together three years ago. They trained Natalia and put her in their act. Six months ago, Hayden and Natalia started dating."

Nancy asked, "Would you say Natalia's as good a flyer or better than Katrina?"

"Katrina's a seasoned performer. Her tricks are clean and controlled," Joseph said.

"But Natalia's younger and more exciting to watch," Eduardo added. "She's gutsy. She's determined to do the triple in the show this year. She's already done it in practice."

"That's three somersaults before the catch," Eduardo put in. "It's a really tough trick."

Joseph nudged his brother. "We'd better get back to polishing our bikes."

When the Pomatto brothers had gone, Nancy said to her friends, "Sounds like Katrina's got a couple of reasons for wanting Natalia out of the way."

"Nobody likes having her boyfriend stolen," Bess said.

"Or losing her star status," George added.

Nancy thought for a moment, then glanced at her watch. "We've got half an hour. Let's go see Lieutenant Green."

Nancy and her friends found the police station with the help of a city map. At the mention of Carson Drew's name, Lieutenant Green was friendly and helpful. Nancy left the towel and the tissue. She gave him the number of the motel where they were staying, then drove back to the circus grounds.

The big top, standing now, dominated the lot.

The men were raising a sideshow tent next to it.

"It's after eleven. We'd better hurry," Nancy said, leading the way toward the trailers.

Just then Marshall Keiser rode past in a dusty old circus truck. He jolted to a stop and backed up. "Nancy Drew, I want to talk to you!"

Startled by his tone, Nancy asked, "Is something wrong?"

Keiser glowered at her from the lowered truck window. He jabbed an accusing finger at her. "What's this about you jumping Katrina at the cookhouse?"

Nancy replied in a level voice, "I asked her some questions about this morning's accident, if that's what you mean. You heard about Natalia's fall, didn't you?"

Impatiently Keiser said, "I heard. And I don't like her making excuses for her falls instead of taking responsibility."

"It wasn't an excuse," Nancy protested. She told him about the towel and tissue she'd dropped off to have analyzed.

Keiser's jaw tightened. "None of my people would purposely cause an accident." He shifted the truck into gear and added, "Nerves are jittery enough around here. I won't have you stirring up trouble between my performers. Stick to looking for Natalia's father and leave the circus to me!"

"He sure was quick to take Katrina's side," Bess said indignantly after the truck was gone.

Nancy nodded. "It's obvious from the way he talks about Natalia that he's angry," she mused. "I wonder why?"

"Angry enough to oil the bar?" George asked.

Nancy shrugged. "Who knows? It doesn't seem likely he'd sabotage his own circus. And it could just as easily have been Katrina who fell."

The three girls resumed walking. Could Keiser be involved? Nancy wondered. Suddenly a possible motive occurred to her. "Maybe he's got a lot of insurance on his key performers."

"You mean, he'd stand to make some money if one of them got killed?" George looked doubtful.

"Right. It's called a key man policy," Nancy said. Her boyfriend, Ned Nickerson, worked for an insurance company during the summer between college terms. She'd learned a lot about insurance from him.

Hanging plants bloomed beneath the awning that shaded the entrance to the pink trailer. Hayden invited them in. Nancy's gaze skipped from the Russian lace covering the tabletops to the colorful curtains and carpet.

Hearing voices, Natalia sat up on the plush red sofa and rubbed the sleep from her eyes.

"How are you feeling?" Nancy asked.

"Much better." Natalia swung her feet to the floor. "I'm sorry about that awful scene this morning, Nancy. We're polishing a new act. Tempers run short."

Nancy said, "You had a right to be upset.

There was something on the bar." She told Natalia about the towel and the tissue.

"I knew I didn't imagine it!"

"Does Katrina dislike you enough to oil the bar?" Nancy asked quietly.

Natalia frowned. "She resents me, for sure."

Nancy hesitated, not wanting to upset either Hayden or Natalia, then said, "Hayden, someone at the cookhouse told me that you and Katrina were a couple for quite a while."

Hayden flushed as he admitted, "Yes, that's true. In fact, we joined Grand Royal together. We were having a lot of problems, though, and we broke up. Then I started seeing Natalia."

Nancy noticed the tender glance that passed between them. She said to Natalia, "It would only be natural for her to resent you for that. Then, there's your talent as a flyer. Do you think Katrina feels threatened?"

"She shouldn't," Natalia said, looking uncomfortable. "She's very good, too."

"Katrina is jealous, though," Hayden said. "It's just the way she is."

Nancy had no more questions about Katrina at the moment, so she changed the subject. "Let's talk about your father, Natalia. What made you decide to look for him?"

Natalia's brown eyes took on an eager glow. "I've always wanted to know about him. I want to know what he looks like and how he met my mother and if he was there when I was born. Oh, so many things I want to know! It's like a hole inside of me. But who could I ask, except my mother?"

"You mean your adoptive mother?" Bess asked.

Natalia nodded. "My birth mother was a ballerina. She died only a day after I was born."

Seeing the sadness on Natalia's face, Nancy felt a pang. She, too, had lost her mother. "And then you were adopted?"

"Yes. By Vera and Piotr Petronov."

"How did you come to America?" Nancy asked.

"Piotr was a performer with the Russian Circus," Natalia explained. "Mother—Vera—was a costumer. Three months after adopting me, they came here on a tour."

Hayden took up the story. "Unfortunately, Piotr was killed in a performance in New York."

"How awful!" Bess exclaimed.

"Mother didn't want to go back to Russia," Natalia told them. "So she defected and found a job with the Grand Royal Circus."

Vera sounded like a very strong woman. "I'm looking forward to meeting her," Nancy said.

Natalia's dark lashes swept down. She said quietly, "Mother's afraid I'll get hurt if my father turns out to be someone—unpleasant. She refuses to help with the search."

"I see," Nancy murmured.

Natalia continued in a soft yet firm voice, "But now that I'm eighteen, I have a legal right to my birth records—if I can find them, that is."

"Do you have any information to go on?" Nancy asked. "Adoption records? That sort of thing?"

"I was born in Moscow. If Mother has adoption records, she's never shown them to me. But I have these," Natalia said. Carefully, she lifted a scrapbook and a frayed shoebox off the coffee table. "They belonged to my birth mother."

Nancy knew by the worn edges of the book and the tape holding the box together that these possessions were Natalia's greatest treasures. Handling them with care, she asked, "Is there a chance Vera knows who your father is?"

"If she does, she's kept it a secret all these years. Even when I was little, she became impatient when I asked about him," Natalia said, her voice quivering with emotion. "I stopped asking because I didn't like to upset her."

Hayden draped a comforting arm around Natalia's shoulders. "The truth is, Vera doesn't want to share Natalia. She gave us a hard time when we fell in love. It was only when Natalia and I threatened to leave Grand Royal and find work with another circus that she agreed to let us date."

"That's so romantic!" Bess sighed. "I'll bet you would have done it, too."

Natalia smiled into Hayden's eyes. "It would have been hard. But, yes, I would have done it."

Nancy drew a single, faded ballet slipper out of the worn box. There was a tiny scarlet *I* embroidered on the satin fabric.

"That was my mother's," Natalia explained. "Her name was Irina Latynina." It rolled off her tongue like a melody.

"That's a lovely name," said Nancy.

"It's beautiful," Natalia agreed. "And it helps a little, knowing something about her." Tears welled in her eyes. "But I don't even know my father's name! Mother says a father who abandons his child has a heart of stone, that I'm better off not knowing him."

Nancy opened the scrapbook. The first few pages were full of newspaper articles, all of which were written in Russian.

"Maybe there's some information in here that could help us find your father." Nancy glanced up. "Do you read Russian?"

Natalia shook her head. "But Mother's read the clippings to me many times over the years. They are all dance reviews. No personal facts— nothing about a husband or a romance," she added wistfully.

Nancy continued thumbing through the book. George and Bess looked on, too. It was frustrating, not to be able to read the articles. Nancy was nearing the end of the scrapbook when suddenly she stopped short.

There was a picture of a woman being helped from an American car by a chauffeur. The brief article below it was written in English.

Nancy looked from the picture to Natalia and back again. The resemblance was striking. "This is your mother, isn't it?" she asked.

Natalia nodded.

Nancy put her finger on the dateline. She did some quick mental math and raised her eyebrows. The article had appeared in *The Washington Post* eighteen years and nine months earlier. "Your mother must have become pregnant with you while she was in America," she said, thinking aloud. "In fact, your father might even be an American!"

Chapter

Four

THAT'S WHAT I hope," Natalia said as Bess and George crowded closer to Nancy to see Irina's picture. She was a beautiful woman with high cheekbones, a firm chin, and deep-set eyes.

"That would sure make it easier to find out who Nat's father is," Hayden said.

Nancy pored over the article. " 'Ballerina Irina Latynina visits Washington, D.C., as the Bolshoi Ballet continues its tour of American cities,' " she read aloud. The article recapped some reviews from the cities in which the ballet had already performed.

"That was big news—especially nineteen years ago, during the cold war," Nancy said. "Why is this the last entry in the scrapbook? I'd think there'd be zillions of pictures and reviews."

"Irina must have been so busy dancing and

practicing and sightseeing, she didn't have time to keep up her scrapbook," Natalia reasoned. "I'm that way too. Mementos pile up for months before I get around to organizing them. I like having something in common with her," she added with a sweet smile.

Nancy turned back to a picture from a Soviet newspaper. It was of Natalia's mother with a handsome Russian dancer.

"Your father could have been someone with the ballet company," Bess suggested.

"I've often searched the photographs, looking for a resemblance to myself in all the men's faces," Natalia admitted. "But I can't see it."

"A ballet troupe is bound to be close-knit. Like circus people. They date other kinkers," Hayden said. "That's the way it was with my parents. And now Natalia and me."

"'Kinkers'?" Nancy said, puzzled.

Hayden grinned. "That's circus talk for performers. My parents were both flyers, too. It's part of me. Circus folks call that getting sawdust in your shoes."

Nancy turned back to Natalia. "You can't rule out the possibility that your father was someone Irina met in the States," she said. "I'll call the newspapers in the cities listed in this article. They can check their morgues, then fax copies of any articles they ran on the Bolshoi while your mother was touring."

"'Morgues'?" Hayden repeated.

Nancy chuckled, realizing the word was as foreign to him as "kinker" was to her. "That's what they call their warehouse for past papers. They're all stored on microfilm."

"I'm really glad you're helping us, Nancy," Natalia said. "I'd be hopeless at this."

Hayden glanced at his watch. "We'd better be going, Natalia. You have to practice again."

Natalia nodded. "Let's just get something to eat before we start."

"Better let me bring you something. Cooky spent the morning cleaning." Hayden added to Nancy, "About a year ago, Nat had a really serious asthma attack. It was right after Marshall Keiser cleaned the carpet in his office. She's learned to be careful of cleaning agents."

"What kind of boss is Mr. Keiser?" Nancy asked.

"He respects kinkers who do their jobs right. But he's kind of thin-skinned," Hayden said. "And he holds grudges."

"He has a good heart," Natalia protested.

"You couldn't prove it by me," Hayden said.

"You don't know him like I do, honey," Natalia said gently.

Hayden shrugged. "A word of warning, Nancy. Watch out when he clenches his cigar between his front teeth! It's a sure sign he's in a foul mood—and he'll take it out on anyone who gets in his way."

"Thanks for the advice," Nancy said. She

looked at Natalia. "Now, where can I find Vera? I'd like to ask her a few questions."

"Mother left just before you came. She wanted to do the laundry."

"We'll come back later, then," Nancy said.

Before heading out the gate, Nancy turned and took one last look at the big top. The workers had gone to lunch, leaving behind a maze of wires and electrical cables. The electrical generator beside the tent made a loud, steady humming sound.

"We still have to check in at the motel," Nancy said, "and then eat lunch. After that, we'll come back. Maybe Vera'll be home by then. I'd also like to look in on the Angel Wings' practice session and see how they get along after that blowup this morning."

The motel where the girls were staying overlooked Sarasota Bay. It was beautifully landscaped with palm trees and lush tropical plants. There was a pool and a private beach. Nancy was relieved to find that the motel offered fax service. Bess, who had overpacked as usual, was happy with the huge closets in their room.

The girls ate a quick lunch in the motel coffee shop. Then Nancy phoned a friend of her father who worked at immigration. Stephanie Cole had attended college with Carson Drew, and they'd kept in touch over the years.

After some coaxing, Stephanie agreed to bend

the rules a little and check the files for information on Vera Petronov. Nancy wanted to make sure Vera was a legal immigrant. If she wasn't, that might explain much of her reluctance to dig into the past.

Stephanie promised to call Nancy as soon as she had anything to report. Nancy's next call was to a friend in her hometown, at the River Heights Library in Illinois. He agreed to fax her the names and phone numbers of the major newspapers in the American cities mentioned beneath the scrapbook picture.

By the time the girls returned to the circus grounds, it was midafternoon. A canvas marquee had been added to the front entrance of the big top. Bleachers, riggings, and props were being carried inside.

Nancy caught a glimpse of Marshall Keiser amidst all the milling workers. His cigar jutted out from between his front teeth. "Uh-oh," George said. "He must be in a bad mood. Let's not take the shortcut across the grounds."

As they followed the road around, a dark-haired woman came toward them, leading a dappled colt. Nancy recognized the woman from one of the circus posters in the arena. She was Hilary Luttrelli, one of a family of bareback riders.

"Excuse me," Nancy called. "Can you tell me where to find the wardrobe mistress?"

Hilary pointed out a trailer parked on the far

side of the arena. Nancy thanked her and continued on past the animal barn with its pungent smell of hay and manure. A dog act was working in the outdoor ring, and some tumblers were using a seesaw board to build a three-man-high pyramid. But the girls didn't have time to stop and watch.

"Would you two check in on the flyers while I go see Vera?" Nancy asked. "See how the three of them are acting. Whether there're hard feelings or if they're being professional. Okay?"

"Okay," Bess agreed. George nodded.

"I'll come as soon as I've talked with Vera," Nancy added.

Nancy knocked at the screen door of the circus wardrobe trailer. A voice called, "The door is open."

The tiny trailer was filled with racks of clothes. Nancy worked her way between them, admiring their gaudy splendor. There were glittering costumes of magenta and gold, pink and red, and yellow and lavender. There were velvet capes and majestic hats with huge ostrich plumes. A brilliant green tuxedo hung on a rack of men's costumes. Rhinestones and sequins flashed from the lapels.

At the back of the trailer, Nancy found a stern-faced woman with iron gray hair and the blackest eyes she'd ever seen.

"I've got a friend who would go crazy over these beautiful costumes!" Nancy said, smiling.

The black eyes narrowed as the woman searched Nancy's face. "Can I help you?"

"I hope so. I'm Nancy Drew."

"The detective?"

At Nancy's nod, the wardrobe mistress said in a cold voice, "I have much work to do."

"I won't stay long," Nancy said quickly. "I just wanted to ask you a few questions."

"As I have told Natalia, I know nothing about her father. Nothing." Vera turned and sat down at a sewing machine with her back to Nancy. She pushed red velvet fabric beneath the foot-feed. The motor whirred as she stitched a seam.

"Mrs. Petronov, it would be helpful if I could see the adoption papers," Nancy tried again.

"They were lost in a fire." Vera bent over and clipped a thread. The snip of the scissors had a ring of finality to it.

Studying her profile, Nancy saw that Vera Petronov was pretty, though her expression was severe.

"Do you think Natalia's father was with the ballet?" she asked.

Vera glanced up from her work, her expression wary. "Why do you ask that?"

"Natalia lent me her scrapbook. I know Irina became pregnant in America." Nancy saw Vera's eyebrows raise just slightly. She added, "Her closest contacts and friends would have been fellow troupers."

"That proves nothing. Where are those men

now? Scattered all over Russia. All over the world, perhaps, now that there is more freedom."

"Perhaps," Nancy agreed. "But I have to start somewhere."

"It would be better left alone. Tell Natalia no, you can't help. Go home."

Nancy outlined her plan to locate more articles about the troupe's tour. She was hoping Vera would see it was pointless to try and keep her from investigating and simply tell her what she wanted to know. "That should give me a list of the performers who traveled with Irina. There may even be mention of the stage crew and whoever else traveled with the troupe," she added.

For a moment Vera's hands stopped. Then, clip, clip, clip went the scissors in the silence of the trailer.

"Mrs. Petronov, I know this has to be difficult," Nancy said gently. "And I understand you may think Natalia's better off not knowing her father. But after all, it's Natalia's choice."

Vera said nothing.

"I don't mean to offend you," Nancy continued. "But I have the feeling you know more than you're telling."

Vera still said nothing. Frustrated by her silence, Nancy ventured, "It was a legal adoption, wasn't it?"

Vera's face turned bright red. She clenched her

fists and demanded, "What do you think, that I stole her? It was legal, of course it was legal!"

"Then why won't you help her? She's dreamed of finding her father for a long time."

"To find him, not to find him. It is not for you to say. I am her mother! I know what is best!"

"Best for whom?" Nancy said in a level voice. "Best for Natalia? Or best for you?"

Vera lurched out of her chair, scissors in hand. She gestured wildly and cried, "You leave it alone, do you hear me? You meddlesome girl. I will fight you. I will fight you with my last breath!"

Then, suddenly, Vera lunged toward Nancy, the scissors still in her hand.

Chapter

Five

Was the woman insane? Nancy thought wildly. Backing away, she said, "Mrs. Petronov, put those scissors down before someone gets hurt!"

Vera stopped short. She looked at the scissors, then flung them down. Her hand trembled as she pointed to the door. "You go now. Out!"

Had Vera really intended to harm her? Or was she so upset that she hadn't realized the scissors were in her hand? Nancy wondered as she hurried from the trailer to the arena entrance.

Bess and George were just coming out of the arena. Hayden and Natalia were with them. They were both drenched in sweat, but their faces glowed with pleasure.

"Nan, you should have seen it!" George said.

38

"Hayden was practically juggling Natalia and Katrina. They passed in midair!"

"That was a passing trick. We really nailed it this time," Hayden said proudly.

Nancy glanced at Hayden. "Katrina behaved herself, then?"

He nodded. "I guess she realizes that with a show coming up, we can't afford to let our differences get in the way of the act."

Bess poked Nancy in the ribs and said in a low voice, "Here comes Bonnie Luttrelli. Her mother's Hilary, the one with the horses. Bonnie's a showgirl. She was inside practicing, too, and she showed me some steps." She waved enthusiastically. "Bonnie!"

A pretty teenager with long blond hair and deep dimples walked over, and Bess introduced her to Nancy. "Are you thinking of joining the circus, like Bess here?" Bonnie joked. "We could use a few new showgirls!"

Nancy laughed. Bess sighed enviously. "I'd love to be in the circus. You get to wear gorgeous costumes and dance, and everyone's looking at you. What fun!"

"That's what you're supposed to think," Bonnie said. "The truth is, it's hard work. Right now, my feet are killing me."

They began walking toward the trailers at a leisurely pace. Katrina came up from behind and passed them. A few steps on, she stopped and turned. "Bonnie? Tell Tom I'll meet him in the outdoor ring at eight tomorrow morning."

"Okay, I'll tell him," Bonnie said.

Katrina looked Nancy up and down. Then, without saying another word, she turned and hurried to a blue trailer that was hooked up to an old truck. Still mad, thought Nancy. How long did she carry a grudge? And how far?

"Katrina and my brother Tom have been working on a stunt, using horses and Katrina's black labrador, Hugo," Bonnie said, when Nancy questioned her. "It's your basic damsel in distress routine. Tom kidnaps the bareback rider—Katrina. As they gallop around the ring, Hugo runs up a ramp and leaps across the horse, knocking Tom to the ground and saving Katrina."

"So Katrina rides, too?" Nancy asked. Seeing Hayden exchange glances with Natalia, she added, "What's she doing—getting an act ready in case she can't make the grade anymore as a flyer?"

"In small circuses many of the performers do more than one thing," Hayden said. "There's a lot of doubling up. A clown could also be a tumbler, for instance. Some of the performers also do technical stuff, like electrical work. They earn more money that way, and the circus can travel with fewer people. So Katrina does two acts.

"But," he went on, "as far as Katrina being a

flyer, she should have a few more years left. But after thirty it gets tough." He kissed Natalia's cheek. "Got to run. I'll see you all later tonight."

Nancy was still thinking about Katrina. Even though the woman could do other things, was Katrina worried that her flying days might be numbered? It seemed that age, not Natalia, was her enemy. And maybe Katrina wanted one last chance to have the spotlight on her alone.

"Is anything happening around here tonight?" Bess asked as Hayden disappeared into his camper.

"Oh, yes!" Bonnie exclaimed. "We're having a big bash over on Siesta Key. It's our annual hit-the-road party."

"Please come! Hayden and I have a surprise," Natalia put in, her eyes twinkling.

The girls accepted, then headed back to their motel to get changed. On the way, Nancy told Bess and George about her visit with Vera. She was hoping that Stephanie had called about Vera's immigration file. But there were no messages for her at the motel desk.

For the party Nancy dressed in white jeans and a blue cotton blouse that set off her reddish blond hair. George wore an Indian-print shirt over black trousers, and Bess decided on a pink minidress and pink flats.

Siesta Key was a barrier island connected to the mainland by two bridges. The fifteen-minute ride was a pretty one. Trees were draped in

Spanish moss. Sea oats, a lovely waving grass, grew along the shore.

"There's the circus truck," Bess said as they approached a paved parking area that overlooked a dazzling white beach.

Nancy parked, and the girls climbed out. The sun sparkled off the ocean in rosy rays. She inhaled the mingled scents of saltwater, woodsmoke, and hamburgers sizzling on a grill.

A crowd was gathered around Hayden and Natalia at the water's edge. Suddenly a cheer rang out from the crowd, and people started hitting Hayden on the back.

"What on earth . . . ?" Nancy began, hurrying to join the others. The clowns she'd met that morning at the cookhouse had shovels and were digging a trench as quickly as they could. Sand was flying everywhere. Sweat was streaming down Packrat's pointy chin. Long-limbed Slowpoke kept shoveling steadily.

Then Jiffy and Dillard nudged Natalia to one side and grabbed Hayden. The crowd howled as Winky and Tim joined their clown buddies in throwing Hayden into the trench.

Sand flew fast and furious as the clowns tried to hold Hayden down long enough to bury him. Eduardo spotted Nancy and her friends and waved them over to the other side of the melee. Bonnie Luttrelli and Joseph were with him. "Hayden and Natalia are going to be married!" Bonnie called.

"So that's the surprise Natalia was talking about," George said.

Eduardo laughed and pointed. "This is the clowns' way of telling him his life is over."

What was Katrina's reaction to Natalia and Hayden's engagement? Nancy wondered, looking around for the redhead. She saw her backing away from the clowns and the flying sand. She walked past the spot where Eduardo, Nancy, Bess, and George were standing. "I didn't get all dressed up just to have sand thrown at me," Katrina grumbled.

"The clowns are just celebrating Hayden and Natalia's engagement," Eduardo argued.

Katrina stopped and regarded him coldly. "I thought this was a season-opening party, not an engagement party."

"Engagement party! Good idea," Eduardo said as she marched away.

Nancy turned and nearly collided with a gray-eyed man. His dark hair was close-cropped, and his pale shirt and shorts showed off his tan. He appeared to be in his late twenties. "Oh, sorry!" he said. "I was trying to get out of the way of the sand."

A shout went up from the crowd. Nancy turned back and saw that the clowns had buried Hayden up to his neck. She grinned as Natalia got down on her knees and kissed him. Then the clowns dug him up again, and the crowd began to break up.

"Hey, Nan! They're putting up a volleyball net on the beach. Want to play?" George asked.

"In a while," Nancy replied. "You guys go ahead. I'll catch up with you."

As Nancy's friends sped down the beach, the man who'd bumped into her asked, "Are you with the circus?"

"No. My name's Nancy Drew."

"The detective?"

Nancy raised her eyebrows. "Now, how does everyone know that?"

"If you know how to listen, you can learn a lot," he said mysteriously. Then he grinned. "So how's it going? Any leads on Natalia's dad?"

Nancy laughed. "If you're so good at finding things out, I don't think I need to tell you."

He held out a hand. "I'm Richard Smith."

"You're not a performer, are you?" Nancy asked, thinking that with his tailored clothes and executive-style haircut, he'd look more at home in a boardroom or a businessmen's club.

"No. My father owns Sunshine Enterprises in Saint Petersburg," he answered. "We lease transport vehicles—this season, to the circus. I came to make sure everything's in good shape before Grand Royal takes to the road."

"I see."

Richard stooped to pick up a shell. Nancy saw, as he turned it in his hand, that the inside glimmered like rainbows on a puddle.

"That's a pretty one," she said.

44

"It's yours." He pressed it into her hand.

"Thanks. I'll take it home to add to our housekeeper's collection."

"Just one shell?" he said, as if she were suggesting giving someone just one glove. "Take her a bunch. To get the best ones, you have to look right after the tide has gone out. But we can try our luck now, if you'd like."

"Yes, I would," Nancy said. As they headed toward the beach, Richard said, "I've always liked shells. I've been collecting them since I was little. My mother used to say everyone ought to collect something."

There was a poignancy in his tone that told Nancy his mother was no longer living. But she didn't feel she knew him nearly well enough to ask about it.

Suddenly the roar of a motorcycle pulling into the parking lot caused them both to turn.

Marshall Keiser parked his motorcycle, climbed off, took off his helmet, and lit up a cigar. He settled it loosely to the side of his mouth and walked over to them. "Evening, Richard. Nancy. How's the party?"

"Nice. And the food smells great. I'm hungry enough to eat a horse," Richard said as Nancy nodded a greeting to Keiser.

"Then what are you doing hanging around here? Go get yourself a plate," Keiser said amiably. He started toward the area where the food had been set out.

"Would you excuse me, Richard?" Nancy asked.

"Of course," Richard said, sounding slightly disappointed. "See you later."

Nancy hurried to catch Keiser. "Mr. Keiser!"

He glanced back and stopped. "What is it?"

"I was wondering how long you've known Vera."

"Almost eighteen years," he replied. "She needed help, and I needed a wardrobe mistress."

"Is she a naturalized citizen?" Nancy asked.

Keiser scowled. "Ask her yourself." He resumed walking.

Nancy hurried to keep up. "One more thing. Do you carry life insurance on your employees? Especially ones with high-risk acts, like the flyers?"

Nancy steeled herself as he scowled at her. He jerked the cigar out of his mouth. "If you're thinking I had something to do with Natalia's fall this morning, you hold that thought right where it is. Because if you go putting it into words, I'm liable to get mighty angry. Understand me?"

Nancy met his narrowed gaze without flinching. "I wasn't accusing you of anything. All I'm trying to do is find out what caused Natalia's fall."

"And I'm trying to put a show on the road with fifty-odd kinkers who are edgy enough without your questions and insinuations!" he shot back.

"But it wasn't an acci—" Nancy began.

He cut her short, jabbing the air with his cigar as he thundered, "This is the last time I'm warning you! No more questions!"

He jammed the cigar between his front teeth, then pushed past Nancy. She watched him march away, his angry strides leaving deep prints in the sand.

Now, what is he so mad about? she wondered. What am I missing—or what's he hiding?

Chapter

Six

Hearing a shell crunch, Nancy spun around. Katrina was standing there. "Marshall's not going to let you disrupt things," she said. "He loves this circus."

"Then why isn't he more concerned over the oiled bar?" Nancy demanded.

"He doesn't believe you. Neither do I," Katrina added with a tight smile.

"Katrina, if Natalia had been hurt, there'd be no act. You must know that."

Katrina shrugged. "It's as good as dead anyway. Natalia is leaving for Ringling when her contract expires in midsummer."

Nancy was taken aback. No one had said anything to her about this!

"It's a big secret," Katrina went on, seeming to

take pleasure in Nancy's surprise. "But I saw the letter myself. I went straight to Marshall and told him. I figured he had a right to know."

Nancy realized Hayden must have been speaking of the Ringling Brothers when he mentioned they'd received an offer from another circus. Mulling it over, she watched Tim the clown lighting lanterns in the twilight. He waved and came over.

"Burgers are done. Who wants to escort me to the table?" he asked with a big grin.

"I will," Katrina said.

Tim flushed with pleasure as Katrina slipped her arm through his. "You'd better come, too, before the food disappears," he called to Nancy as they started away.

"I'm coming," Nancy said. She trailed behind, thinking, Ringling Brothers! Wow! That explained Keiser's anger with Natalia. He didn't want to lose her. But why didn't he seem angry with Hayden, too?

Hayden and Natalia were filling their plates at the food-laden table. However, there were too many people around for Nancy to ask about the Ringling offer. She decided to wait until later.

But Nancy never did get a chance to speak privately with Natalia and Hayden. Just then George, Bonnie, and Eduardo led a sopping Bess up to the food table. "A wave got her," George told Nancy. "I think we ought to get her back to the motel—the night air is pretty chilly."

"I'm okay, really," Bess protested. But she was shivering.

"Don't be ridiculous," Nancy scolded gently. "You look like you're about to freeze solid."

"Go home before you catch a cold. We've still got tomorrow night," Eduardo said.

"T-t-tomorrow n-night?" Bess echoed, teeth chattering.

"Sure. We've decided to throw an engagement party for Natalia and Hayden. You're all invited, too," Eduardo said.

"We're there," Bess said promptly. Nancy saw Eduardo's delighted grin. Obviously, he had a crush on Bess.

Bonnie, Joseph, and Eduardo waved as the three girls drove away. On the ride back to the motel, Nancy told Bess and George about Keiser's warning as well as what Katrina had said about Natalia's plans to leave the circus.

"Well, that explains why Keiser is mad at Natalia. He won't like losing her." George echoed Nancy's earlier thoughts.

Nancy nodded agreement, wondering just how much he would hate it. Enough to see Natalia injured rather than go to a rival circus?

Back at the motel, there was a message for Nancy from Stephanie and a fax from her librarian friend. In their room Nancy read the message. "Stephanie says immigration has no record of a Vera Petronov."

"How can that be?" Bess asked, peeling off her wet clothes.

"It's not so surprising, really," Nancy said, thinking. "Vera probably changed her name when she defected. I'll ask Natalia."

As Bess went to shower, Nancy scanned the fax. The old *Washington Post* article naming cities where Irina's troupe had already toured had proved helpful. Her friend listed twenty newspapers as well as phone numbers, all of them in the East, where the tour had begun.

"We should be able to track down some articles with this—and maybe some clue to Natalia's father's identity," Nancy added. "I'll start calling first thing in the morning."

But the next morning, Lieutenant Green phoned with the results of the lab test and gave Nancy something else to think about. The smudges on the towel as well as the tissue had turned out to be medicated petroleum jelly.

"I'm going to see if Katrina has any petroleum jelly in her trailer," Nancy said as they waited for Bess to finish drying her hair.

"What if she catches you?" Bess asked.

Nancy glanced at her watch. "It's almost eight now. I'll make sure she's busy practicing with Tom Luttrelli before I let myself in. I also need to start phoning these newspapers," she added, fax list in hand.

"Why don't we split up?" Bess suggested. "I'll make those calls. I'm good on the phone."

"You've had lots of practice, that's for sure," George said, and they all laughed.

Twenty minutes later, Nancy and George were at the circus grounds, leaning on the low fence that encircled the outdoor ring. There were eight horses, galloping in pairs, with four riders standing on the backs of each pair.

George watched intently, admiring the skill of one young Luttrelli as he did a backward flip and landed on the next pair of horses, right in front of his brother. "Think of the balance that takes! Tumbling skills seem to be part of nearly every act at the circus," she marveled.

Nancy nodded. The beating of the horses' hooves alone was enough to get the adrenaline flowing! She would have liked to watch longer, but the case was her first priority.

"Katrina's not here. Let's check the arena," she said. They set off past the barn with its animal medley of camel grunts, elephant trumpeting, and the growls and roars of lions and tigers.

Hayden and Natalia were in the arena warming up. "Where's Katrina?" Nancy asked, after greeting them both.

"We're a little early," Hayden pointed out. "She's working with the Luttrellis until nine."

"We were just there, but we didn't see her," George said.

Hayden shrugged. "Maybe she overslept."

Nancy told them about the lab results. They

had no idea how the medicated petroleum jelly could have gotten on the bar.

"Have there been other accidents? Anything suspicious at all?" Nancy asked.

They both thought it over. "No," Hayden said finally, and Natalia agreed.

Nancy moved to her next question. "Natalia, did Vera change her name after defecting?"

Natalia said, "Not that I know of. Why?"

Nancy shared her theory that Vera's strong opposition to the search for her father might be a result of a secret she was trying to hide, such as staying in the country illegally.

"No, that can't be. She told me that after her defection, Marshall helped her seek asylum with the U.S. government. She's a citizen." Natalia said confidently. "I'm sure of it."

"Immigration has no record of her," Nancy said. "Not under that name, anyway."

"That's strange," Natalia said. "Or maybe it isn't," she added, after a moment's thought. "She wouldn't tell me if she had changed her name. She's very secretive about a lot of things."

"Has she always been that way?" asked Nancy.

"Always." Natalia added softly, "I think it's because she grew up in a country where people had to be so careful of what they said."

"Because of communism, you mean?" George asked, and Natalia nodded.

Nancy decided not to press it. Natalia was clearly hurt by her mother's secretiveness. Instead, she asked, "Is it true that Ringling Brothers has offered you a contract?"

Natalia exchanged a startled glance with Hayden. "Yes," she said after a moment. "Hayden and I both received letters."

"Six months ago, when Vera was trying to keep us apart, we videotaped an aerial performance and sent it to Ringling," Hayden told Nancy and George. "This past week we both got letters offering us positions."

"Are you planning to accept?" asked Nancy.

"It's a great opportunity," Hayden said. "But Natalia's spent her life with Grand Royal. She needs time to think it over."

"I've put off telling Marshall about the offer—I know he won't like it," Natalia said.

"What do you mean?" Nancy asked.

"Well, I like to think he'd be happy for me. But at the same time, I know it'd be a blow to Grand Royal. The act has really helped bookings."

"Mr. Keiser already knows," Nancy said, and recounted her conversation with Katrina.

Anger flashed in Natalia's eyes. "Of all the mean—! No wonder Marshall's been so touchy with me!"

"But how did Katrina know about the offer?" Hayden asked.

"She says she saw Natalia's letter," Nancy said.

"But I've kept my letter in my sports bag ever since I got it," Natalia protested. "Katrina couldn't have seen it—unless she went through my things!"

Hayden's face darkened. "She had no right!"

"It *is* pretty crummy," George agreed.

"She's gone too far. I'm going to confront her right now!" Hayden started away.

"I'm coming with you," Natalia said, hurrying after him toward the exit.

Nancy and George followed the two flyers past the barn to the ring where the Luttrellis were still practicing. Katrina was nowhere in sight.

"Natalia!"

Nancy turned to see Hilary Luttrelli waving to Natalia. The loud whine of a motorcycle drowned out the rest of Hilary's words.

Natalia hesitated a moment, then turned back toward the fenced-in ring and said to Hayden, "I'll catch up with you."

"Look!" George exclaimed, pointing to a steel globe rolling down the road toward them. "It's the Sphere of Death! The guys must be practicing."

Nancy's eyes watered as the sun flashed off the steel sphere. The loud rev of the engine hurt her ears.

Hayden, banging on Katrina's trailer door twenty feet ahead, didn't give the globe a glance. Neither did Natalia, who was twenty feet behind, talking across the fence to Hilary.

But George and Nancy were mesmerized. The

rider handled the ball deftly, making accurate turns, weaving to the left, then the right. He was clad in black leather and a black helmet, his face completely covered by the face shield.

"Is that Eduardo or Joseph?" George asked as the ball rolled past them.

"Who could tell in that gear?" Nancy replied.

The ball slowed. The motorcycle engine idled, as if the rider was holding back.

Nancy turned to watch the globe round the corner and roll past the outdoor ring. Natalia waved as it passed and moved away from the fence. She was about ten feet away from Nancy and George when the globe turned and came back.

The driver opened the throttle. The engine screamed as the ball rounded the corner and came toward Natalia. He'll turn, thought Nancy. Any second now, he'll swerve. But, boy, is he cutting it close!

Suddenly the hairs on her neck prickled. He was *too* close. He was going to hit Natalia!

Chapter

Seven

N ATALIA!" Nancy screamed. She lunged at the girl, pushing her with such force that they both hit the ground and rolled. The Sphere of Death whizzed past, leaving them dazed and coughing in a cloud of dust.

"Nan!" cried George, rushing to her side.

"Don't move them! They may be injured!" Hilary Luttrelli shouted.

As Nancy's head cleared, she saw Hilary and her sons racing from one direction as Hayden came running from the other. White and shaken, he dropped down beside Natalia. "Natalia! Sweetheart!"

Nancy drew a deep breath and sat up, relieved to see Natalia unhurt and in Hayden's arms. She dusted herself off and squinted into the sun, looking for the ball. "There he goes, out the gate. Who was it, George? Did you see?"

"He kept his helmet down. It could have been anyone," George said.

"Let's get the car and go after him."

The girls took off at a run. As they passed Eduardo's trailer, he came bounding around from the back. He was obviously distraught.

"Someone stole my motorcycle! Someone stole the sphere!"

"We're going after it!" Nancy cried.

Eduardo was right on Nancy's heels as they tore through the gate. There they stopped short. The Sphere of Death, trap door open, had been abandoned in the paved parking lot.

"Maybe we can still catch the guy," Nancy said. They all piled into her rental car. Nancy rammed the key into the ignition and turned it, then backed out of the space and screeched toward the street.

"There he is! That black speck, two blocks down!" George exclaimed.

The tires squealed as Nancy turned onto the street. She pushed the accelerator down. They were gaining on him. He was only a block ahead now—she could see the motorcycle clearly.

"He's turning left, Nan," George advised.

"Turn, too! Maybe you can cut him off!" Eduardo cried from the backseat.

Nancy pulled hard on the wheel. The tires shrieked as she made the turn. She gripped the wheel hard and accelerated. At the next block she turned right. The street, lined with palms, ran parallel to the beach. At the intersection she looked up the street to her right. The cyclist should be coming straight toward them, she thought.

But the street was empty.

"We lost him!" Eduardo cried.

"He must have doubled back," Nancy said. She drove half a block and stopped. "There! That's where he turned."

The gravel at the edge of a driveway had been thrown in a wide arc as the motorcycle had spun around and doubled back. Nancy sped to the next corner, but there was no motorcycle in sight.

"Gone!" she exclaimed in frustration.

"Whoever it was, he got away with my bike," Eduardo said in a mournful voice.

"Could it have been Joseph?" Nancy asked.

Eduardo snorted. "Why would my own brother take my bike?"

"And he wouldn't have ridden straight at Natalia like that," George added.

"It was deliberate, no question," Nancy said.

"What are you talking about?" Eduardo demanded.

Nancy told him about Natalia's near accident. In the rearview mirror, she saw Eduardo's eyes widen in astonishment. "It's beginning to seem as if someone really does want to hurt Natalia," he murmured.

"Marshall Keiser rides a motorcycle," Nancy said quietly.

Eduardo looked shocked. "Sure. But riding inside the Sphere of Death isn't like riding a street bike. It takes lots of practice."

"What about Katrina?" Nancy pressed on. "Does she ride?"

Eduardo stared. "Katrina? She's a girl."

"So what?" George retorted. "She rides horses. She's strong. She has a good sense of balance. She could do it, with some practice."

"I've known Katrina for three years," Eduardo said, "and I've never seen her ride."

"Do you think Katrina is angry enough about losing Hayden and her star status to take revenge?" Nancy asked. She watched Eduardo in the rearview mirror. He was frowning.

"I don't know," he said.

"What about Keiser?" asked Nancy. "Would he hurt Natalia?"

"No way! A lot of people come to the circus just to see the aerialist act. That's money in Marshall's pocket!"

"What if he thought Natalia was going to leave?" Nancy pressed. "What then?"

"He wouldn't hurt her. It was probably some daredevil who's seen the act and wanted to try it for himself," Eduardo said. "And steal my bike in the bargain," he added.

Nancy pulled into the circus parking lot. She could understand why Eduardo didn't want to believe anyone was trying to kill Natalia, but as far as she was concerned, the evidence was clear.

The steel globe was still in the parking lot. Joseph and the Luttrelli boys were checking it over while a woman Nancy didn't know looked on. She was in her thirties and slender, with large glittery-framed glasses and dangling earrings.

"Who's that?" Nancy asked as the woman turned and walked onto the circus grounds.

"Morgan York, our performance director. She'll be walking us through the rehearsal this afternoon," Eduardo explained.

The moment Nancy parked, Eduardo was out of the car. He raced over to the globe, with Nancy and George following.

Nancy examined the globe. Essentially, it was a round cage. The door could be opened either from the inside or the outside. But, she thought, the cyclist would have to get the thing stopped to get out. It would definitely take skill.

She beckoned to George. "Let's see if Katrina ever showed up. Then we'll find out where Marshall was when the accident occurred," she said. They started through the gate.

Hayden and Natalia were in the arena, practicing without Katrina.

"How can she cut practice like this?" George asked.

Nancy looked at her watch and was surprised to see it wasn't even nine yet. "She's still got ten minutes."

Bonnie Luttrelli was alone in the outdoor ring as they passed on their way to Katrina's trailer. Nancy called from the path, "Why aren't Katrina and your brother practicing the rescue act?"

"Tom's horse stepped on something, so the boys are working with the other horses while the vet looks at Ranger's foot. Where's Bess?"

When Nancy told her Bess was still at the motel, Bonnie grinned and resumed shoveling the ring, saying, "And here I was ready to turn this glamorous job over to her!"

Nancy waved, and the two girls walked on. "What now?" George asked.

"We've wasted enough time. Let's check Katrina's trailer," Nancy said. She led the way to the door. No one answered her knock.

"I'm going to slip around back," Nancy said. "If Katrina or anyone else comes along, start talking loudly, okay? That'll be my signal to clear out."

"Are you sure you should do this in daylight?" George said uneasily. "What if someone sees you?"

Nancy spread her hands. "I can't waste any more time. I've got to see if Katrina has some of that medicated petroleum jelly. And if she was the one in the globe, maybe she left something lying around that'll give her away."

George nodded. She walked over to a white poodle tied up in front of the next trailer and scratched his neck, trying to look casual as she kept watch.

Nancy went to the back of Katrina's trailer. She noticed a chain encircling a scrubby pine tree. That was probably for the dog, she thought. She slipped up to the back door and tried it. It too was locked. The trailer was quiet. If the dog that went with that chain was inside, he wasn't much of a watchdog.

Nancy brushed past a garbage can, then stopped short. A piece of pink fabric was sticking out from beneath the lid. Curious, she removed the garbage can lid and took out the pink sash Katrina had worn the day before. There was a shadowy stain on it—the kind of stain petroleum jelly might make.

Nancy looked carefully at the sash. Katrina could have doubled the sash over, then concealed a wad of petroleum jelly within the fold. It had probably soaked through the sash.

Nancy dug through the garbage. Stuffed into a bag of half-rotted lemons was a plastic jar of petroleum jelly! Marked on the lid were the words Medicated Petroleum Jelly. Nancy put the container and the sash in her shoulder bag. She had her proof.

She was retracing her steps toward the front of the trailer when she heard voices. She peeked around the corner. Katrina was back! She had a huge black labrador leashed at her side.

"You should have seen that globe barreling down on her! It's a wonder Natalia wasn't killed!" George was talking very loudly.

Nancy flattened herself against the trailer. She looked around, planning how she could get away without Katrina seeing her. Katrina's backyard ended at the fence that enclosed the circus grounds. She thought about climbing the fence but then realized the top of the fence was tall enough to be visible from the front of the trailer. Katrina would see her climbing over.

Just then a menacing growl interrupted Nancy's thoughts. She peeked around the corner of the motor home again. The labrador's ears were standing up. He strained at the leash and barked.

"What is it, Hugo?" Katrina asked, stooping to pat him.

As she did so, the dog jerked the leash right out of her hand. With a ferocious baying, he came galloping toward the end of the trailer where Nancy was hiding.

"Your dog!" George yelled.

As if in slow motion, Nancy saw the dog leap . . . saw his white teeth gleam in a snarl . . . felt the heat of his breath. In another second, he'd be upon her!

Chapter

Eight

Nancy swung her bag with both hands. It deflected the animal. He backed off with a startled yelp, then came at her again. Fear zinging through her veins, Nancy swung her bag a second time.

Katrina ran around the side of the trailer. "Down, Hugo! Down!" She stamped on the free end of his leash. The dog jerked up short, unable to reach Nancy.

Nancy leaned shakily against the trailer. George raced to her side as Katrina dragged the dog over to the tree and hooked him to his chain.

The labrador quieted at Katrina's command and sat down. "Now, you stop that. Stop that growling!" she said firmly. Leaving him chained to the tree, she came back to Nancy and George.

"He's trained to act mean, but he wouldn't have hurt you. What are you doing here, anyway?" Katrina demanded, eyeing Nancy coldly.

"You didn't answer your front door. I thought maybe you didn't hear me, so I tried the back door," Nancy said, thinking fast.

Katrina's eyes narrowed. "Snooping, huh?"

Nancy ignored the question and asked one of her own. "Katrina, do you know how to ride a motorcycle?"

"No. And I don't have time for your questions —I'm late for practice," Katrina added.

"We'll walk you there," Nancy said quickly.

Katrina shrugged and unlocked her door. When she came back out, she had her athletic bag.

"Was Natalia hurt?" she asked.

"No. But I think it was a deliberate attack. Where have you been for the past half hour?"

Katrina stopped in front of the outdoor ring and leveled an angry stare at Nancy. "Are you accusing me?"

"Do you have an alibi?" Nancy shot back.

"Why would I need one?" Katrina demanded.

Nancy folded her arms. "You hate Natalia. You read her mail. You told Marshall Keiser about the letter from Ringling, making it sound as if Natalia had already accepted. And then you caused her to fall from the trapeze."

"You can't blame me for that. She missed her

trick, that's all." Katrina resumed walking. Her strides were long.

Nancy kept pace. "She missed her trick because you greased the bar with petroleum jelly."

"That's crazy!"

"Is it?" Nancy reached into her shoulder bag for the sash and the jar of petroleum jelly. "I found these in your garbage."

Katrina's jaw dropped. Then she blustered, "You had no right to dig through my garbage! I'll tell Marshall! He'll throw you out!"

Nancy called her bluff. "Do that," she said. "But first, you should know the towel Natalia wiped her hands on yesterday had petroleum jelly on it. I had the smudges analyzed at the crime lab. I can take this sash to the lab, too, and have these stains analyzed." Nancy pointed out the blotches. "I think the results will be conclusive—even in Mr. Keiser's eyes."

Katrina said nothing. Her face was pale.

Nancy folded the sash lengthwise and tied it around her waist. "The way I figure it, you hid a dab of jelly right here," she said, sliding her finger into the space between the folds. "Then you climbed up the ladder. While the rest of us were talking below, you greased the bar."

"Natalia went first. I didn't touch that bar," Katrina said.

"Yes, you did," Nancy said, knowing it was time to push. "I saw you. You held the bar without swinging out on it. Then, when practice was halted, you said you were going to the cookhouse. But you didn't go straight there, did you?"

Katrina looked away, but Nancy didn't let up. "You went home and changed first. You couldn't risk someone noticing the stain on your sash. That's why you were late getting to the cookhouse."

Katrina's mask cracked. "All right, so I did it," she said. "I didn't want to hurt her badly or anything. I just thought if she landed wrong, she might sprain her wrist. Then Hayden and I could do the show alone, just like we used to." Her voice broke. "I wanted him to see that the act didn't have to end just because Natalia was leaving. He still had me."

So Katrina didn't know about Hayden's offer from Ringling! Hiding her surprise, Nancy pressed, "And this morning?"

"You can't pin that on me!" Katrina exclaimed, clearly alarmed. "I was walking Hugo on the beach."

"Did anyone see you?" asked Nancy.

"I don't know. I don't think so." Katrina's voice trembled, but she looked Nancy right in the eye. "But that's the truth. Really."

Nancy stared at her for a long moment, then opened the arena door and held it for her. "They're waiting for you inside."

The door closed behind Katrina. "What do

you think?" George asked, squinting in the sunlight.

Nancy sighed. "I think we can't rule out Katrina. But we can't rule out Mr. Keiser either. He has almost as good a motive as Katrina, and we don't know what his alibi is."

"But he won't answer your questions. So how can we find out?" George asked.

Nancy gazed at the big top, where someone was working on sound equipment. Crackling, popping sounds spilled out over the grounds. Was Keiser in there? Had anyone seen him yet this morning? she wondered. Starting across the grass, she said, "Maybe someone else can tell us."

Nancy led the way to the back door of the tent. The sun filtered through the red-striped top, casting a rosy glow on the ring in the middle of the tent. The smells of canvas, sawdust, and animals hung in the air.

The girls paused to watch a team of Hungarian acrobats who were practicing on a teeterboard. A dark-eyed man gave Nancy a gold-toothed smile and gestured, saying, "You try, pretty lady?"

"No, thank you. I'm looking for Mr. Keiser." He shrugged and went back to work.

Just then Nancy caught the eye of Morgan York, the performance director. Morgan left the crew at the sound board and strode over.

"Looking for work? You'll have to talk to Marshall Keiser," she said, blinking at them from behind her glittery-framed glasses.

"Where can we find him?" Nancy asked without setting her straight.

"He's not here. He's buying parts for the sound equipment. Can't afford new. Low cash flow," Morgan said, speaking in choppy phrases.

Nancy and George left through the back. Nancy waited until they put a little distance between themselves and the big top before saying, "If Mr. Keiser was out shopping when the attempt was made on Natalia's life, maybe a clerk will remember him. We can check that out later. Right now I'd like to see about that insurance theory."

"Didn't Mr. Keiser tell you he didn't have life insurance on his performers?" George said.

Nancy had dealt with enough crimes to know never to take what a suspect said at face value. "He could be lying. If the show needs money fast, Natalia might be worth more to him dead than alive. Or it could be revenge. Or both. Maybe he figures that if she's leaving anyway, he might as well murder her. That way he'd have money *and* he'd have revenge. And since Mr. Keiser doesn't know yet about Ringling's offer to Hayden, he may be thinking that as long as he has Katrina and Hayden, he's still got an act," Nancy reasoned. She opened the arena door.

In the main corridor, Nancy knocked on the door with Keiser's nameplate on it. No one answered. Nancy stepped back and assessed the lock with a practiced eye. "Piece of cake. Stand right here and knock if anyone comes."

George nodded.

Nancy took a credit card from her wallet. After glancing up and down the hall, she slid the card between the plate and the lock and jiggled the card. The lock popped open, and she slipped inside and closed the door.

The office was dusty and cramped. There was a desk, some wooden chairs, and a number of filing cabinets. Nancy crossed to several tall closet-type cabinets crowded against one wall and flung open the doors. The first one was empty except for a dusty top hat, a sequined jacket, and a half-used container of carpet cleaner. The second was full of props and sound paraphernalia. The third contained old record books. Alert for George's warning knock, Nancy moved to the filing cabinets.

The filing system was alphabetical. She had no problem finding the file labeled Insurance. There were no key man life policies, though. Nancy was about to close the cabinet and leave when another idea occurred to her.

The old record books! Were any of them for payroll? If so, how far back did they go? Far enough to list Vera's real name? Or had she changed it even before asking Keiser for a job?

It was worth checking. Nancy scanned the cabinets. There were a dozen payroll books, so dusty they made her cough. Keiser kept thorough records, she thought. The books went back twenty years.

Quickly Nancy sorted through, finding the one from eighteen years earlier. The entries were self-explanatory. Date, name, type of service rendered, amount paid out. Hastily Nancy flipped through, looking for payouts to wardrobe employees. There were none until September.

The entry leaped out at her. "Vera Neverenko, Wardrobe, $100.00 paid in cash." Neverenko! Vera *had* changed her name, Nancy thought. She shoved the books back into the cabinet. Then, after making sure she left the office just as she'd found it, she slipped back out to the hallway, where George was waiting anxiously.

On the ride back to the motel, Nancy filled George in. Once at the motel, they stopped at the registration desk to ask if any faxes had come in.

The woman behind the desk smiled at the girls. "I've got a pile right here."

"Great!" Nancy picked them up and started away. But the woman called her back.

"Miss Drew! I almost forgot! Someone left this for you." She handed Nancy a white envelope.

Nancy's name was typed on the front, but there was no address. She tore it open and pulled out a postcard.

A prickly sensation crawled up her spine as she saw a tombstone on the front with her initials typed on it. On the back, a typed message read:

"N.D. A little knowledge is a dangerous thing. Stop asking questions if you know what's good for you."

Chapter

Nine

WITHOUT A WORD Nancy handed the card to George. Who would send such a warning? Marshall Keiser? Katrina? Vera?

George gave a low whistle. "You're making someone very nervous."

"But who?" Nancy studied the card. "The typing is bad. Only two sentences and I count seven errors. And look at this." She pointed out a letter *l*. "Every *l* is raised half a line."

Nancy turned back to the desk clerk. "Did you see who delivered this card?"

"I'm sorry, I didn't. I stepped away from the desk a moment. When I returned, it was here." The clerk smiled apologetically.

Nancy put the card on top of the pile of faxes, then followed George to their room. Bess was just hanging up the phone.

"Perfect timing. I just finished my last call," she said.

Nancy held up the pile of faxed articles. "Bess, you're a treasure. There must be fifteen or twenty articles here."

Bess beamed. "Talking's my specialty. But all that talking made me hungry."

George went to get carryout food for their lunch, while Nancy and Bess got down to work. First, Nancy called Stephanie Cole and gave her Vera's real last name. Perhaps now Stephanie would be able to locate some information on Natalia's adoptive mother.

Next, Nancy and Bess divided the faxed clippings. Nancy went through her pile, scanning photos. Most were taken during performances. Faces were blurred and tiny. Disappointed, Nancy started through the pile again, reading each article.

Suddenly Bess yelped, "Hey! Look!" She held out a fax showing a photograph of Irina stepping out of a limousine in Times Square. The chauffeur was helping Irina out. The headline read, "Soviet Dancer Visits New York."

It was so similar to the clipping in Natalia's scrapbook that Nancy thought for a moment it might be the same one. But no. That clipping had come from *The Washington Post.* This was from *The New York Times,* and the shot was clearer. But the car certainly looked like the same one!

Nancy thought. Perhaps even the driver was the same, though she couldn't be sure.

The chauffeur was smiling. Irina's head was thrown back, her eyes flashing with laughter. Who did those eyes remind her of? Nancy wondered.

"Natalia looks like her mother," Bess remarked. "I'd die for cheekbones like that. And look at that chin!"

Of course, Nancy thought. She should have recognized the resemblance. She peered more closely at the photo and felt a tingling of excitement as she saw that the license number was legible, although not the state.

Just then George came back. "Dig in," she said, setting hamburgers, french fries, and soft drinks on the table.

"I'm going to call Phillip Green first," Nancy said, reaching for the phone.

"Why?"

Nancy showed George the clipping. "I'm hoping he can trace this license number through the Department of Motor Vehicles."

Bess's eyes shone with excitement. "You think they can trace the chauffeur?"

"I know it's a long shot," Nancy said. "But we've got so few leads in this case. I'm willing to try anything."

By the time Nancy got off the phone, her fries were cold. But Lieutenant Green had agreed to run the license number through the Department of Motor Vehicles in New York City and in Washington, D.C., since the photographs had been taken in those two cities. Because the photograph of the limousine was so old, he'd warned her it might take a while.

Nancy quickly ate, then said, "Let's go back to the circus before the two o'clock rehearsal. I want to tell Natalia about Katrina's confession to oiling the bar. And we'll take the faxes. First, though, let's make a copy of the one with the chauffeur." Something about it nagged at her, as if there was something she was missing.

The girls hurried to the lobby and got the copy made. Nancy tucked it into her bag. Moments later they were on their way to the circus.

As Nancy drove, she pulled the postcard out of her pocket, thinking of the typewriter in Keiser's office.

"It isn't clear what questions are making your secret pen pal here uneasy," George said, reaching for the card. "Is it your search for Natalia's father? Or your questions about the attempts on Natalia's life?"

"Vera's the only one who's objected to my searching for Natalia's father," Nancy said. "Keiser strikes me as a more face-to-face kind of man, though he was gone from the grounds this morning. So he had opportunity. Then there's Katrina. But it would have been hard for her to have delivered the note to the motel."

"She could have sent someone else," George pointed out. Nancy nodded—that was true of all the suspects.

The other thing she had to keep in mind was that the two cases could be related. It was possible that, for some unknown reason, someone out there was willing to kill to keep Natalia from finding her father.

It was one-fifteen by the time Nancy and her friends knocked on Natalia's door. Dressed for the rehearsal, she looked elegant in a brief white costume and fishnet tights.

"I know you don't have much time," Nancy said. "But I wanted to tell you that Katrina confessed to oiling the bar."

After Nancy recapped her conversation with Katrina, Natalia said angrily, "Maybe it's best if Hayden and I accept Ringling's offer. After this, working with Katrina is going to be impossible."

"Have you told Vera about the offer?" Nancy asked.

"I told both Mother and Marshall today at lunch," Natalia said. "Mother was proud and sad and happy, all at once. She knows it's a golden opportunity. Yet she hates to be left behind."

"What did Mr. Keiser say?" Nancy asked.

"He grumped around. Once he gets mad, it takes him a long time to get over it." Natalia sighed. "I can't believe Katrina oiled that bar! How do I know she won't try it again?"

"She knows we're onto her," Nancy pointed

out. "She'd better make sure you *don't* get hurt because she's the most obvious suspect."

"Maybe all three of you should sit down with Mr. Keiser and hash things out," George said.

"That would be a good idea, unless Keiser is involved in the case, too," Nancy said.

"Marshall wouldn't hurt me," Natalia said quickly. But her face grew even longer as she added, "But then, a few days ago, I didn't think Katrina would, either."

Natalia had every right to feel frightened, Nancy thought. "Maybe you shouldn't perform again until we find out who's behind these attacks."

"I can't do that," Natalia said. Her expression intense, she added, "That's not what the circus is about. No matter what happens, the show must go on. I'll just have to be extra careful."

"That's dedication," George said, smiling.

Nancy nodded at Bess, who had the faxes of the newspaper clippings. "We thought you might like to see these."

A flush of excitement colored Natalia's cheeks as she accepted the faxes. Instantly engrossed, she didn't even look up when Nancy said, "I need to look at your scrapbook. There's a picture I want to see again."

"Help yourself. It's in that closet at the end of the hallway," Natalia said.

Nancy hurried down the hall and opened the

closet door. The first thing she saw was an old black typewriter.

Glancing back to make certain Natalia wasn't watching, Nancy slipped the postcard out of her pocket and into the typewriter. She hit several keys, then hit the letter *l*. It came out perfect. She hit the key a few more times to make certain, then rolled the card out. If Vera had sent the threat, it wasn't from that typewriter.

Nancy took the scrapbook down off the shelf and rejoined her friends on the sofa. She took out the copy she had made of the article with the close-up of Irina and the chauffeur. Then she opened the scrapbook to the *Post* picture, comparing the two to see if the car and chauffeur were the same. They were!

"You mean the same man drove her for the whole tour?" George asked. "I would have expected a different limousine service for every city."

"If it was the same man, he may remember my mother!" Natalia cried. "He may even know who she was seeing."

"That's what I'm hoping," Nancy said, and went on to tell Natalia about having the license number traced.

"Nancy, thank you so much! I never could have done this alone!" Natalia's eyes shone with hope. "What a precious find these articles are. Thank you, thank you so much for all of these."

"Bess is the one to thank. She spent the whole morning on the phone," Nancy said.

Natalia hugged Bess. Then she stood up. "It's almost two—I'd better go. By the way," she added, smiling, "there's an engagement party tonight for Hayden and me. Eduardo will use any excuse to throw a party. He's a good guy. But he's really down over his stolen motorcycle, and I'm hoping the party will take his mind off it. You'll all come, won't you?"

"We never miss a party," Bess assured Natalia as they followed her to the tent.

Inside, Nancy nearly butted noses with a woman who had a huge snake coiled around her upper body. "Excuse me," Nancy said, backing away.

In the tent, workers were busy leading show dogs, carrying props, and checking cables, ropes, and wires.

Natalia shot off to join Hayden, Katrina, and some other performers who were waiting on the bleachers. "Why didn't you tell her about Vera's real name?" George asked quietly.

"Finding out you don't even know your mother's real name isn't all that pleasant," Nancy answered. "There's the rehearsal, then the party tonight. I'd hate to upset her right now."

Just then Morgan York shouted into a megaphone, "Attention, please! We've got sound problems here, so listen up!"

As the noise leveled off, Morgan rushed through a roll call. Only one man failed to answer. Morgan frowned, made a note on the paper on her clipboard, then continued. "Mr. Keiser will say a few words first. Then we'll bring the animals in and practice the walk-around."

So Keiser would be occupied for a while. Nancy knew there would never be a better time to check the typewriter in his office. She beckoned for her friends to follow and ducked out.

"This is only going to take a second," Nancy tried to reassure Bess as she approached Keiser's office, credit card in hand. "Stand outside and warn George if anyone comes toward the arena."

"I'll knock if anyone does," George said, stationing herself outside Keiser's door as Nancy let herself into his office.

Nancy closed the door and crossed to Keiser's desk. She moved a stack of papers off the old standard typewriter, rolled in her postcard, and typed several letters, including the letter *l*. The nerve endings in her fingers tingled. The letter was raised half a line! A perfect match!

Hearing something bump against the wall that separated Keiser's office from the prop room, Nancy jerked to attention. Her pulse surged as George knocked on the door. She raced to the window and slid it up.

The screen was stuck! It must have been painted over, she thought.

George's second, more urgent knock sent Nancy hurrying across the office to hide in the first tall cabinet. Then came footsteps. Her heart pounded as she hid behind a sequined jacket. The dusty smell of it made her nose itch. Oh, no! she thought. She was going to sneeze. She covered her nose with both hands. But it was no use. The sneeze exploded.

Marshall Keiser's bellow rang out. "I hear you in there! What do you think you're doing?"

Chapter

Ten

NANCY CRINGED. Marshall Keiser had said no more questions. Breaking into his office had to be ten times worse. Pulse racing, she waited tensely for him to throw the cabinet door open.

But the door remained closed. Nancy listened hard. She heard voices coming from the prop room. Keiser was still bellowing—but not at her!

Relief rushed through her. The cabinet door creaked as she opened it. Wincing, she tiptoed soundlessly to the office door and opened it, checked to make sure there was no one in sight, and slipped out.

George had crossed the corridor so as not to give Nancy away. She was studying the circus posters. Her feeling of relief was obvious on her face as she turned and saw Nancy. In silent agreement, they raced out the front door.

"Where is he? I thought for sure he'd catch you!" Bess cried, her eyes wide with concern.

"He went into the prop room. From what I could hear, that guy who didn't show up for roll call was in there taking a nap. He was getting a good chewing out," George said.

"Let's get out of here before he sees us and gets suspicious," Nancy urged. She led the way back to the big top, climbed the nearest set of bleachers, and sat down.

They had missed the animals and performers marching in and parading before the audience of workers. The ringmaster was on the elephant drum, announcing the acts in his own special spiel.

Nancy wiped her forehead. It was hot in the tent. The heat seemed to be draining the circus people, too, for they were slow-moving and short-tempered. Morgan barked over the megaphone, "Get the lead out, girls! Smiles, I want smiles!"

Showgirls kicked, strongmen flexed, clowns juggled, acrobats tumbled and flipped while in the background the small band played. In the midst of it all, Nancy told Bess and George about the *l* on Keiser's typewriter.

"Then he *did* send the postcard!" Bess exclaimed.

"Not necessarily," Nancy said, thinking it over. "Someone else could have used his typewriter. With or without his knowledge," she added, thinking of how easy it was to break into his office.

"The whole business just doesn't feel right," Nancy went on after a minute. "Threatening me to my face, now that was his style. But an unsigned note . . ."

"I see what you mean," George said. "But if it wasn't Keiser and it wasn't Vera, that leaves only Katrina."

"Or it could be someone we haven't even considered. With a motive we haven't thought about yet," Nancy added.

George nudged her. "Here comes that guy you were talking to at the party."

"Nice tan," Bess added in an undertone, as Richard Smith started up the bleachers.

Nancy returned Richard's smile. He looked trim and cool in tan slacks and a pale yellow shirt open at the neck. Nancy wished she looked as fresh as he did. She introduced him to her friends and said, "I didn't expect to see you today."

"My dad and I took over the Grand Royal account just two months ago from another firm," Richard explained as he sat down beside her. "We want Mr. Keiser to know the service will be as good or better than what he was getting before. I dropped by to make sure everything's going smoothly."

"Oh, poor Eduardo!" Bess said. The cyclist was walking toward them, shoulders slumped. As he approached, riggers were securing the steel mesh globe in ring two. As they stepped back, Joseph rode in the back door on his motorcycle, up a ramp and into the Sphere of Death.

"And now, in ring two, daringly executed by Joseph Pomatto, fifty dizzying, death-defying revolutions within the Sphere of Death!" cried the ringmaster, waving his arm dramatically.

Nancy's pulse hammered along with the drum roll. A showgirl secured the trap door. Joseph revved the motorcycle engine and started making high-speed circles within the globe.

"Haven't the police found your motorcycle yet?" Richard asked Eduardo as he joined them.

"No, unfortunately," Eduardo said. Nancy looked at Richard out of the corner of her eye. He was very well informed for an outsider.

Morgan called, "Okay, that's good, Joseph. Clear the ring. Intermission. Clowns? Where're my joeys? Let's see some walk-arounds!"

"You have only one bike?" George asked Eduardo.

"One is all I can afford," Eduardo replied.

"A customized bike like that costs an arm and a leg," Richard put in.

"I don't think whoever stole it wanted the bike itself," Nancy said. "I think the person intended to run Natalia down. He or she probably abandoned it and made a fast getaway. Do you ride, Richard?" she asked, wondering how he knew so much about what Eduardo's bike would cost.

"I used to, a little. But I messed up my knee pretty badly about ten years ago. The doctor who put it back together warned me it wouldn't take any more abuse," Richard replied.

Nancy gazed at him a long moment. But then she dismissed the idea of his involvement. He had no reason to want to kill Natalia—he didn't even know her. Nancy couldn't go around suspecting every person who'd ever ridden a motorcycle.

"I hope it turns up," Eduardo was saying. "It isn't just the money, it's our act. What's the thrill of one guy in the sphere? Two of us in there, looping around just missing each other by inches, now *that's* entertainment! That's what the audience wants to see. If that bike doesn't show up, Marshall Keiser may cancel our act."

Bess patted Eduardo's shoulder. "I'll bet Nancy's right. Someone will find it and return it to you."

Eduardo changed the subject. "You're coming to the bash tonight, aren't you?" he asked Bess.

"Wouldn't miss it," Bess said, smiling.

"Great!" Eduardo flashed a grin. Turning to Richard, he added, "Feel free to drop by."

As Richard accepted, Nancy glanced at her watch. "We'd better go back to the motel. By the time we've gotten ready, it'll be time to come back for the party."

But what she really wanted to do with the time

was call some sound shops and see if anyone remembered that Keiser had been there that morning.

They bid Richard and Eduardo goodbye and left the tent. Bess looked puzzled as they started for the gate. "It's not even four o'clock, Nan. The party isn't until seven."

Nancy explained her plans. Besides, she was finding it hard to think clearly in the midst of all the commotion, and she did need to think. She was no closer to learning who'd tried to run down Natalia than she'd been moments after it happened.

The moment she returned to the motel, Nancy headed for the phone. She called every single sound shop in the Sarasota yellow pages, but no one remembered Keiser. Discouraged, she took a shower. She had just stepped out and pulled on her robe when Phillip Green called. As she listened, Nancy towel-dried her hair.

"The report on that license number just came in," he told her. "The limo changed hands a number of times. But nineteen years ago, it was licensed to Victor Bykov of Manhattan."

Nancy grabbed a pen and took the address.

"It's been a long time. Bykov probably has moved," Green warned. "And even if you do track him down, what can you learn from him?"

Nancy explained about the two clippings with

Bykov's picture. There was something in the way the chauffeur and the dancer were laughing together that made her hopeful they'd been friends. He might know whom she'd been seeing. Perhaps he had even driven them places.

After she finished talking to the lieutenant, Nancy dialed Manhattan information and asked for the phone number of Victor Bykov and gave the address. The operator said there was no listing for a Victor Bykov at all—at any address. Nancy bit her lip. A dead end.

Glancing at her watch, she saw it was time to get dressed for the party.

Bess was standing at the closet, trying to decide what to wear. "How about this coral-colored dress?" she asked.

"It's a great color on you," Nancy said.

As the girls were dressing, the phone rang again. Nancy reached for it and was excited to hear Stephanie Cole's voice on the other end of the line.

"According to the file, Vera Neverenko entered the country eighteen years ago," Stephanie said. "It says here she was traveling with the Russian Circus. Several years later she applied for and received American citizenship."

"Then she *is* legal. Natalia said she was," Nancy said. "But what's she so afraid of? Is there more?"

"The file lists two people who entered the

country with her. Piotr Neverenko, her husband, and an infant by the name of—let's see, I wrote it here somewhere . . . Natalia Bykov."

"Bykov?" Nancy caught her breath. "Did you say Bykov? But that means—" She lowered the phone in astonishment.

It meant that Natalia's father was Irina's chauffeur!

Chapter

Eleven

NANCY THANKED Stephanie for her help and hung up. When she told her friends what she'd just learned, Bess shrieked, "You did it, Nan! You found Natalia's father!"

"Not yet. But I do know who I'm looking for," Nancy said. "It was in the picture all along. That shared laugh. The way they were looking at each other."

"How did Irina and her chauffeur get separated?" Bess asked.

"Irina had to return home with her ballet company," George pointed out.

"She could have defected as Vera did," Nancy said, thinking out loud. "Though it wouldn't have been easy. Vera, by the way, is a naturalized citizen. And I think I know now what she's been trying to hide."

Bess looked puzzled. "I don't."

"Natalia's name was listed as Bykov. Vera didn't adopt her. That's why she doesn't have any papers. That's why she changed both their names to Petronov."

Bess's blue eyes were round. "You mean, Vera kidnapped her?"

"No. But I don't think she got her from an orphanage. Maybe Irina and Vera were friends, and Irina asked Vera before she died to care for Natalia." Still mulling it over, Nancy put on a white miniskirt. "She may have chosen Vera and Piotr because she knew they were coming to this country. Maybe she wanted them to bring Natalia to Victor Bykov."

"Then why is Natalia still with Vera?" Bess asked.

"Good question." Nancy pulled on a black, loose-weave sweater and crossed to the window that overlooked the ocean. Gulls soared over water that pitched and tossed like her thoughts.

"Maybe Bykov didn't want Natalia," she said finally. "Or, for that matter, he could have been dead, or married, or lost—any number of reasons. But the way Vera's resisting this search, I'm wondering if she didn't just decide to keep the baby. She could have been hiding all these years from Bykov."

"Wow, that's some story!" Bess gasped.

"So far, that's all it is," Nancy pointed out. "We have to learn the truth."

"But not tonight. Tonight we party." George slipped a sheer white blouse over a sleeveless emerald green top and tied the shirttails at the waist of her white spandex leggings.

Nancy smiled as she slipped into black flats, then fastened a gold chain around her neck. "Ready when you are!"

Hayden and Natalia were greeting guests as Nancy and her friends entered the arena. The rosebud in Natalia's hair matched her pale yellow dress. She looked as graceful as Hayden was handsome in his dark suit. Nancy squeezed their hands and offered her best wishes.

"You two look so good together," Bess said sincerely.

Nancy noticed that the arena floor had been cleared for dancing. One low trapeze bar, left hanging, was decorated with bright pink flowers and purple ribbons.

"Have you set a date yet?" Bess was asking.

"End of the season, I guess. Nat has her heart set on a formal wedding," Hayden said.

"I want Mother in the front row and all of our friends in the pews. What I'd like most of all is to have my father walk me down the aisle," Natalia said softly.

"I'm working on it." Nancy smiled.

Natalia turned to welcome another guest. Bess was tapping her toe to the music drifting from the bandstand set up at one side of the room.

Five men in gold-braided uniforms were playing a medley of love songs.

Richard Smith, looking tan and attractive in white trousers and a pale pink shirt, came up to offer his congratulations. Nancy nodded to him, then turned as Bess nudged her. "Are you going to tell Natalia about learning her father's name?" Bess asked.

"Not tonight," Nancy replied in a low voice. "It raises as many questions as it answers. And besides, Natalia will have to know soon enough that Vera's been lying to her all these years."

"I hadn't thought of that," Bess admitted. She looked disappointed, but a moment later, she nudged Nancy again and whispered, "Look who's here!"

It was Katrina, dressed in a red, snug-fitting satin mini, clinging to Tim's arm. Nancy could see that the clown was proud to be Katrina's date.

"She has some nerve, showing up here after what she did," George muttered.

Just then the gold-toothed acrobat Nancy had met in the tent that day swung into a dance step with a woman a head taller than he. Her dangling earrings tinkled as she danced. The band picked up the tempo. Soon other couples joined in.

"Nancy! You look lovely tonight."

Nancy pivoted to meet Richard Smith's approving gaze.

"Why, thank you! You look pretty nice yourself," she said, smiling.

Richard returned her smile. "Have you managed to collect any more shells for your housekeeper?"

"No," Nancy said. "I'd love to, but I've been too busy."

"Well, how about taking a couple of hours off tomorrow? I check the paper every day for the tides, so I know there's a low tide in the midafternoon and one about four-something in the morning. I've got a meeting in the afternoon, though. Would you like to go before dawn?"

"And collect shells in my sleep?" Nancy said, laughing.

George poked Nancy gently. "Careful," she murmured. "If Ned were here, he'd be getting jealous around now."

"There are Eduardo and Joseph!" Bess's eyes lit up as the Pomatto brothers headed their way.

"Good news!" cried Eduardo. "The police found my motorcycle abandoned in a downtown park."

"It was propped up against a tree. There wasn't a scratch on it," Joseph said.

"That's great!" Bess exclaimed. "See? Sometimes even terrible things turn out okay."

"Do the police have any idea who left it there?" Nancy asked.

"Nope," Eduardo said. "Which means whoever the jerk was, he's going to get away with it."

The music stopped. Nancy looked to see Hayden escorting Natalia to the table that had been set up for refreshments. Packrat stood by the punch bowl, about to make a toast.

A smile on his face, the clown waited as Bonnie Luttrelli and her mother, Hilary, passed glasses to all the guests. Then Packrat lifted his glass. "Marshall isn't here to do the honors, so I've stepped in. Hayden, Natalia, may you fly through life together, never missing a trick."

"And may you have lots of little flyers," Dillard hollered from the dance floor.

The guests applauded as Hayden and Natalia drank to the toast. Then the guests moved toward the food. Nancy and Richard got in line.

"I hear you're making progress tracking down Natalia's father," Richard remarked as the line inched forward.

How did he know? wondered Nancy. She hid her surprise and asked, "What makes you think so?"

"I overheard Bess talking to you a few minutes ago. She said something about your having learned Natalia's father's name." Smiling, he added, "Congratulations to a very clever young lady."

"I've had a few breaks," Nancy said, then changed the subject as she filled her plate with fresh fruit, a vegetable salad, and baked clams.

George and Joseph joined Nancy and Richard at their table. Bess and Eduardo soon came along, with Bonnie Luttrelli and a shy, freckled sword-swallower trailing after them.

There was a table at the head of the room for Natalia and Hayden. Vera sat with them, leaving one empty space. Nancy wondered if the empty chair had been meant for Marshall Keiser. Where was he, anyway?

When everyone had finished eating, the lights over the arena dimmed, and the band struck up a romantic slow dance. Nancy saw Hayden rise from the table and take Natalia's hand. The tender smile they exchanged made Nancy think longingly of Ned. For two people in love, they certainly spent a lot of time apart.

A moment later, as other couples joined them, Richard asked Nancy to dance. His musk-scented cologne tickled her nose as she followed his steps.

"You dance very well," Richard said, and smiled. "Come to think of it, you seem to do everything well."

Nancy laughed lightly. "You don't know me."

"I'm trying," Richard said smoothly. "Which reminds me, you never did say whether you'd go shelling with me in the morning."

He certainly is persistent, Nancy thought. "It sounds like fun, but I don't think I'd better. I'm pretty focused on my work right now," she answered.

The band struck up a fast song with a strong beat. Nancy was about to excuse herself when long-limbed Slowpoke, in dress pants that showed an inch of white sock, cut in. He danced so loosely it was as if he had elastic for limbs. They were both laughing when Jiffy cut in and stole her away.

Everyone else was changing partners, too. Nancy changed so many times, she completely lost track of Richard. She was matching steps with the gold-toothed tumbler when Bess danced by with the lion tamer and said behind her hand, "Look at the clowns. They're up to something."

Nancy saw Jiffy, Tim, Slowpoke, Dillard, Packrat, and Winky drift around to the far side of the tables and stoop down. When Tim stood up again, she caught a glimpse of white passing from his hand to his pocket.

The music changed to a slow song. Nancy's partner escorted her off the floor. The lights dimmed. The spotlight came on, casting a circle of light around Natalia and Hayden. The clowns moved forward in shadow. What were they doing? Nancy wondered, amused and intrigued.

The other dancers fell back, forming a wide circle around the engaged couple. Anticipation mounting, Nancy watched the clowns creep up on Hayden and Natalia, who were too lost in each other to notice. The clowns crept closer and closer. Then they sprang.

Hayden turned in surprise. A shout rattled the rafters. The clowns jerked white balls from their pockets and swung at the lovers' heads. White puffs of dust exploded into the air.

Natalia shrieked. Nancy saw her bury her face against Hayden as the clowns kept pummeling the couple. Then Nancy lost sight of Hayden and Natalia in a cloud of fine dust. But she could hear Natalia wheezing. Gasping. Something was wrong!

"Stop!" Nancy cried. Fear thrust her through the wall of clowns. She reached Natalia's side just as the girl crumpled to the floor.

Chapter

Twelve

"Gᴇᴛ ʜᴇʀ ɪɴʜᴀʟᴇʀ!" Hayden cried, as Nancy helped him lower Natalia to the floor.

"M-my p-purse," Natalia choked out, wheezing and gasping for breath.

Nancy backed out of the way as Vera dropped down beside her daughter and pressed the inhaler into her hand. "Here, darling, here! Calm down, now. Just breathe."

To Nancy's alarm, Natalia's hand fell away, and she dropped the inhaler. Vera scooped it up, then let out a cry. "It's empty! Hayden, run to the trailer. There's another one on the table."

Hayden raced away, leaving Natalia to Vera and Nancy. Nancy knew each second counted. "I'll call an ambulance," she said quickly.

The only phone in the building was in Keiser's office. Nancy took off at a dead run. She popped

Keiser's door open with a credit card, Richard at her heels. Her fingers flew as she dialed the emergency number. A dispatcher answered. Quickly Nancy explained the emergency.

"What's your address?"

"What's the address?" Nancy asked Richard.

"I'm not sure." He shuffled through the papers on Marshall Keiser's desk. "Maybe there's something here with an address on it."

As Richard searched, Nancy said in a rush, "It's Grand Royal Circus Winter Quarters, off Highway Forty-one. I don't know the exact number."

"All right. Stay where you are—we know the location. The unit is leaving right now."

Nancy thanked him and hung up. She turned to Richard, who was staring at a slip of paper he had picked up off Keiser's desk.

"Did you find the address?" she asked.

"No," Richard said slowly. He frowned.

"What's wrong?" Nancy asked.

He seemed hesitant. "It's this post— Never mind. Keiser's correspondence is none of my business. Let's go tell them help is on the way."

"You go ahead. I'll be right there," Nancy said, determined to find out what Richard seemed so anxious to conceal from her.

The moment he'd gone, Nancy reached for the card that had caught his eye. Her throat went dry. A tombstone was pictured on the front, just like the card she'd received. She flipped it over and read the typewritten message: "N.D. You're an accident waiting to happen."

Just then the door banged open. Nancy braced herself for action, but it was George and Bess who came running in.

Nancy held out the card. "Look at this."

"Another card! Where'd you find it?" George asked.

"Richard found it on Keiser's desk. He didn't want me to see it. I guess he thought it would upset me."

"It should!" Bess said, her voice filled with concern.

Nancy returned to the crisis at hand. "How's Natalia?"

"She can't get her breath. Nan, she's in a bad way," George said.

"Didn't the medicine help?"

"Hayden hasn't come back with it yet."

"I'd better go see what's keeping him," Nancy said, striding out of Keiser's office. "You two go to the gate. The ambulance won't know which building to go to when they get here."

The night was dark, with only a few stars overhead. The girls ran past the animal barn and the outdoor ring, then past the row of motor homes. Every dog in the place seemed to be barking. Nancy turned at Vera and Natalia's home while Bess and George raced on toward the front gate.

The trailer was all lit up, the front door standing open. Nancy took the three steps in a single bound. The kitchen and front room had been turned upside down. Hayden came rushing down the hallway. White dust still clung to his clothes and face and hair. He was frantic.

"I've looked everywhere. I can't find another inhaler."

"Where does she keep them?" Nancy asked.

"On the kitchen table. But there's nothing there."

"Easy, Hayden," Nancy said, hearing the panic in his voice. "There's a rescue unit on the way. Go back to the arena. I'll look for the medicine," she added, guessing that in his state, he wouldn't find it even if it were in front of his nose.

"Thanks, Nancy," Hayden said gratefully, and ran out the door. Nancy made a swift search of the kitchen. Nothing. She tried the bathroom medicine cabinet. No spare inhalers there, either.

She raced into Natalia's bedroom and jerked open her dresser drawers, her makeup cases, her closet door. Nothing but shoes and clothes and an athletic bag. Natalia's athletic bag! Nancy grabbed it off the floor and scattered the contents. The inhaler! She worked the thumb squeeze. Yes! It contained medicine.

Nancy glanced at her watch. Ten minutes had passed since she'd called for the ambulance, yet she'd heard no siren. Where was it? Couldn't the driver find them after all?

Nancy grabbed an envelope with the circus

address on it, ran to the phone, and punched in the emergency number again. "This is Nancy Drew at the circus," she said when the dispatcher answered. "I phoned ten minutes ago. Where are you?"

The dispatcher sounded confused. "But I—I don't understand."

"What do you mean?" Nancy demanded.

"Someone called and canceled the unit. They said the girl was being driven to the hospital."

"No!" Nancy cried. "That's wrong, my friend's still here." She gave him the address on the envelope. "Hurry!"

Nancy clutched the inhaler in her hand and ran back the way she'd come, questions racing through her mind. Who could have canceled the call? And what had provoked Natalia's asthma attack? Surely, whatever it was, the clowns hadn't done it on purpose, had they?

As Nancy sped past the wide front doors of the animal barn, she was suddenly jerked off her feet. A gloved hand muffled her scream. A strong arm pulled her inside, into the darkness. She threw her head back, trying to land a painful blow on her attacker's nose, but she hit something hard instead. A motorcycle helmet! The inhaler flew out of her hand.

She kicked and struggled and clawed, but her fingers couldn't penetrate the thick leather worn by her attacker. She was flung to the floor. A knee jabbed into her stomach, holding her down. An oily tasting rag was jammed into her mouth, and a gag was tied over that. Then her assailant bound her wrists and ankles with rope and dragged her through the barn. She recognized the jingle of the shackles that linked the elephants to their stakes.

Her attacker opened another door and dragged her through it. Then suddenly she was flung into a cage. The metal door clanged shut. The smell was terrible—a wild, jungle smell. Her pulse roared in her ears.

She was locked in the tiger cage!

Chapter

Thirteen

KEEP COOL, Nancy ordered herself. She knew that if the tiger sensed fear, he would attack.

There was a thud off to her left, then a snarl. Nancy tensed, but nothing happened.

Then she realized the tiger must be in the cage next to hers. She sagged with relief. Shakily she tried to loosen the ropes binding her. The gag was tight, too, and the oily rag burned her throat.

Patiently she worked at the ropes. As the minutes passed, more cats began to roar. Off in their own part of the barn, the horses whinnied. An elephant trumpeted. Above the roars and trumpets of the animals, a siren wailed.

Natalia! In her own peril, Nancy had nearly forgotten. The siren came closer, then stopped. It was a few minutes before it wailed again. Nancy hoped they hadn't come too late to help.

Who had been hiding behind the motorcycle gear? Marshall Keiser? Or Katrina? No, she was at the party. Or at least, she *had* been, earlier. Nancy realized that she hadn't seen Katrina among those gathered around Natalia.

Suddenly the doors to the barn opened, and a light came on. "What's the matter, kids?" came the soft voice of Burton, the elephant trainer.

"Is something wrong? What's going on?" asked a second voice. Richard! Nancy thought.

"Hold it down," Burton said quietly. "Something's got these critters all stirred up. You wait here."

Nancy followed the beam of a powerful flashlight as it traveled from cage to cage. This whole room was full of caged cats! She shivered as Burton murmured from the door, "Don't seem to be nothin' wrong."

Afraid he'd go off and leave her, she started kicking the cage. A moment later, Burton's shuffling steps came her way. He peered at her in astonishment. "Missy, what happened to you?" Quickly he opened the door.

"What is it? Nancy!" Richard was beside Burton. His hands were gentle as he helped her out. "Are you hurt? How on earth—"

"Cut her free, son," Burton said, producing a pocketknife.

Richard cut the ropes. As he sliced the gag and pulled the oily rag out of her mouth, Nancy spit the terrible taste out. "How's Natalia?" she asked, breathless.

"Not good," Richard said. "Hayden and Vera went to the hospital with her. How did you get in there, Nancy?" He wrapped his arms around her protectively.

Nancy explained what had happened. Shaking a little from shock, she was comforted by Richard's warm embrace. It felt good to be safe.

"Who'd do such a thing?" Richard asked.

"I don't know, but I'll find out." Nancy slipped out of Richard's arms and brushed straw off her clothes. She looked at him. "That postcard you found wasn't kidding, was it?"

"You saw it?" Richard's voice contained a mixture of worry and regret. "I didn't know what to do when I found it. I didn't want to upset you. I never dreamed something like this was going to happen, or I would have—"

"You folks better go so I can get these critters settled down," Burton cut in.

Richard and Nancy headed back to the arena. Most of the guests had left the party. Jiffy, Packrat, and Dillard were washing tables. Eduardo, Joseph, Bess, and George were folding chairs while Tim, Winky, and Slowpoke took down streamers.

Bess was quick to notice Nancy's soiled white skirt. "Nancy! What happened to you?"

"I'll explain later," Nancy said. She asked the clowns, "What was the deal with the socks?"

"It's an old clown gag," Slowpoke said. "White-socking."

"They didn't mean any harm, Nan," Bess said as the other clowns came over to join them.

"It's a joke clowns like to pull to celebrate an occasion. Like a birthday or anniversary," Eduardo added.

Nancy frowned. "What's in the socks?"

"Face powder," Dillard said.

"It's to set our makeup," added Tim. "Every clown has a white sock."

"We socked her on her birthday, and she didn't get sick," Packrat said, looking sick himself.

"Did you use the same kind of powder?"

"Yes," Winky said, blinking a droopy eye. "We all use the same. Always have."

What had triggered Natalia's attack, then? Stress? Suddenly Nancy remembered something Hayden had said about cleaning agents. Maybe there were other substances that would cause Natalia breathing problems.

"Would you mind if I took a look at all your socks?" Nancy asked.

The six clowns untied the knots at the top of their socks. Nancy dipped her hand into sock after sock. The powder inside five socks was satiny smooth, with little odor. But when she put her hand into the last sock, the one belonging to Tim, she felt a difference.

"This is coarse." She examined the tiny particles in her hand and held them up to her nose. "It smells different, too."

George leaned in and took one sniff. "That's carpet cleaner! I'd know that smell anywhere."

An alarm rang in Nancy's head. Carpet cleaner —it had caused Natalia to have an earlier attack. Hayden had said so.

Tim took the sock and examined the white powder closely. "It does smell like carpet cleaner. But how did it get in my sock?"

Nancy said, "Someone put it in there. Someone who knew Natalia was allergic to carpet cleaner—and who wanted her out of the way." She looked at Tim. "When did you use your sock last?"

He looked frightened. "Just before rehearsal today. Nothing was wrong with it then."

"Where's it been since then?" asked Nancy.

"In my trailer. Until I came here and hid it behind the mats."

"Was anyone at your trailer today? During or after rehearsal?"

Tim started to shake his head, then hesitated. "Katrina was waiting outside my trailer when I got back from rehearsal."

Nancy thought of Katrina oiling the bar. Had she done this, too? "Was your door locked?" she asked Tim. He shook his head. "Did you have any carpet cleaner in your trailer?"

"No. I don't have a carpet."

"Did Katrina know you guys planned to pull your sock trick tonight on Natalia and Hayden?"

"Sure," Tim said. "We planned it last night at the beach party. *Everyone* knew."

Nancy ignored that. "Where's Katrina now?"

"She went home when the white-socking started. We got powder on her good dress, and she got mad," Tim said, looking miserable.

"And you guys all left your socks hidden behind the mats, right?"

The clowns all nodded. So, Nancy thought, anyone who knew they were there could have tampered with Tim's sock. Maybe she could get somewhere by tracking down the source of the carpet cleaner. Suddenly she snapped her fingers, remembering that she'd seen carpet cleaner in Marshall Keiser's office earlier that day.

"I'll be right back." Nancy raced toward Marshall Keiser's office. The door was open, and she went straight to the cabinet. Everything was just as she'd left it before—except the container of carpet cleaner was missing.

Bess, George, Eduardo, Joseph, Tim, and Richard came running in.

"Does anyone see a carpet-cleaner container?" Nancy asked.

Within seconds, Bess cried out, "I found it!" She was about to pick the container out of the trash when Nancy cried, "Don't touch it. Maybe the crime lab can lift some prints."

She used a tissue to pick it out. Without the prints of a suspect to check them against, prints on the can would be useless in tracking the culprit. But when Nancy found the culprit—and she wouldn't stop until she did—prints could be taken and proof established.

"Good work, Bess," Nancy said.

"I suppose you'll be wanting this, too," Tim said. He looked like the saddest clown in the world as he gave Nancy his powder sock.

By the time the girls left, it was after midnight. Nancy decided to wait until morning to take the evidence to Phillip Green. On the way back to the motel, she told Bess and George about being thrown in the tiger's cage.

"Nan, that's so scary!" Bess cried.

"It was," Nancy confessed. Smiling, she added, "And smelly, too. I can't wait to get out of these clothes."

"You *are* pretty ripe," George agreed.

As soon as the girls reached their room, Nancy stripped off her skirt and sweater and put on her robe. Wrinkling her nose, she stuffed the skirt in a laundry bag. She was about to put the sweater in the bag as well when she noticed something gold glittering on the sweater. It had caught in the loose weave.

Nancy removed the bit of gold, then held it in her hand and stared at it. "Hey, look! It's the stem of a wristwatch," she said. She held the stem up to the light. Then its significance became clear—and a surge of excitement swept through her.

"It must have caught in my sweater when I was struggling with my attacker," she said. "This little bit of metal may tell us who's trying to kill Natalia!"

Chapter

Fourteen

NANCY WRAPPED the watch stem in a tissue and put it in her coin purse. It was one of the few pieces of hard evidence she had in the case.

"I'll have to come up with a way to check the wristwatches of all my suspects," she said, thinking aloud.

"Nancy," Bess said firmly. "Stop planning for just a little while and get ready for bed. It's been a long day. You need some sleep."

"Yes, Mom," Nancy said, grinning.

She showered quickly and was slipping into her nightshirt when Bess spoke to her from the next room. "I just called the hospital, Nan. Natalia's out of danger."

Nancy came out of the bathroom. "How long before she feels better?"

"Hayden says it's like a bad case of the flu. It'll take her a day or two to build up her strength."

"Good. She's safer in the hospital than up on a trapeze. I've got to find out who's trying to kill her before she flies again," Nancy said.

"Who do you think it is?" George asked.

Nancy shrugged. "The case against Marshall Keiser is getting stronger. He could have ridden the Sphere of Death when it nearly got Natalia—he has the knowledge, and he has no real alibi. Also, he knows Natalia's allergic to carpet cleaner. He could have emptied her inhaler and stolen the spares when he had lunch there today. And then there's the call canceling the rescue unit. I guess he could have made it, then dashed to the barn and grabbed me as I went by, to make sure I didn't get Natalia's medicine to her."

"Sounds possible to me," Bess said.

Nancy hesitated.

"It also sounds as if you don't believe your own theory," George remarked.

"It bothers me," Nancy admitted. She pulled down the sheets and climbed into bed. "That's a lot for one man to do without being seen by anyone. It's almost *too* much evidence. And then there's that postcard. Why would he leave something like that lying around in plain sight?"

"Okay, then, what about Katrina?" George suggested. "We already know she oiled the bar."

"Right," Nancy said. "That's why I can't believe she's behind this other stuff. I mean, she knows we're onto her. She isn't stupid—she knows that if anything more happens to Natalia, she'd be the prime suspect."

"Maybe she's got a partner," George said.

Nancy sighed. "Maybe. Or maybe I'm on the wrong trail altogether. Victor Bykov keeps coming into my head, but I don't know where he fits in. This is so frustrating!"

"Maybe it'll be clearer in the morning," Bess suggested. "Let's go to sleep."

Lying there in the dark, a thought struck Nancy. "You know," she said, "Richard helped me out of the cage. His watch stem could have snagged on my sweater then."

"Should be easy to check," George murmured.

Or when he hugged me, Nancy thought. But he'd been so helpful when she was upset. It was good to have someone there for you when you needed them, she thought, and drifted off to sleep.

Next morning, after dropping off the powder sock and the can of carpet cleaner at the police station, the girls went to the hospital.

As Nancy parked the car in the hospital lot, Bess said, "Look, it's Mr. Keiser!"

Marshall Keiser was striding across the lot, cigar in hand. How could Nancy learn where he'd been the night before without asking questions?

Nancy wondered. Searching for the right approach, she went to meet him.

"Good morning!" she called. "That was a close call Natalia had last night." She sneaked a glance at his watch. It was a digital, with no winding stem.

Keiser looked at his watch, too, and said in his abrupt way, "I don't have a lot of time, so why don't I say it for you? I was in the cookhouse this morning, and the place was buzzing. Someone put carpet cleaner in one of the clown's powder socks. The empty can was found in my office, and you're wondering if I'm responsible." He clamped down on his cigar.

A little taken aback by his directness, Nancy said, "Anyone could have put that can in your office."

Irritably he said, "True. The lock on my office door doesn't work too well. But then, I guess I don't need to tell *you* that."

Nancy blushed, but she didn't bother to defend her actions. Instead, she watched Keiser's face, saying, "If you have any ideas about who may be setting you up, I'd like to hear them."

Surprised, he took the cigar from his mouth and knocked off the ashes. "I settle my own scores. But I'll say this much—I should have listened to you sooner. Natalia's alive today because of you. I admire that. And I'm grateful," he added, the abrasiveness dropping from his manner for a split second.

"Two heads are better than one," he continued. "As long as you don't get underfoot, you've got my permission to question any of my people you think might have had a hand in these attacks on Natalia. Then you come to me, and I'll take care of it. Understand?"

Nancy found herself wanting to believe Marshall Keiser, but she had met too many likable crooks in the past to let her feelings get in the way of logic. She still needed to know Keiser's alibi, if he had one.

"I'll help in any way I can, Mr. Keiser," she said in a neutral voice. Thinking swiftly, she added, "By the way, it was a pretty good party last night, right up to the white-socking."

Keiser narrowed his eyes. In a tone of grudging respect, he said, "I was at World of Sound in Saint Petersburg, if that's what you're asking. Check it out." He nodded curtly, turned, and walked away.

"Wow!" Bess whispered. "Talk about major surprises. What's gotten into him?"

"He's scared about his circus, and he needs Nancy's help," George said.

There was one way to find out. Nancy found a phone in the hospital lobby and looked up the number for World of Sound in Saint Petersburg. The clerk who answered hadn't worked the evening before. At Nancy's insistence, though, she gave the name of a man who had. In less than five minutes, the man had confirmed Keiser's alibi.

"You're narrowing the field of suspects, at least," George said.

"Which means you're getting somewhere," Bess said with an encouraging smile.

The girls made a stop at the hospital's gift shop, then went to the information desk to get Natalia's room number. When they got to Natalia's room, they found that she was sleeping. Vera was at her bedside, napping in a chair. Hayden was in another chair. Seeing the girls at the door, he tiptoed out to the hall.

"It's the first really restful sleep Nat's had," he said in response to the girls' concern.

"Just tell her we were here," said Nancy.

"And give her this." Bess held out the music box with a circus scene on it that they'd just bought in the hospital gift shop.

Hayden's tired expression momentarily vanished as he gave the girls a grateful smile. "Thanks. She'll love it. Let me just put it down." He took the music box into the room and carefully set it on the bedside table. Then he came back out into the hallway.

"Nancy," Hayden said, "thanks for taking charge last night. I don't know what we'd have done if you hadn't been there."

"I'm just glad she's going to be okay," Nancy said.

"If there's anything else we can do, let us know," George offered.

"Actually, there is," Hayden said. "Now that Nat's resting easy, Vera and I could use a ride back to the circus grounds. There's a rehearsal this afternoon. It'll be just Katrina and me, but the show always goes on."

"Sure. We'd be glad to," Nancy said.

"Just wait while I run down to the nurses' station and tell them we're going," Hayden said.

"Okay," Nancy said. "I'll wake Vera." Nancy stepped into the room. Vera's face, in sleep, had lost its sternness. Her features were soft, pretty in a faded way. The high cheekbones, the firm chin, the parted lips were familiar.

Nancy stared at her a moment longer, puzzled by the familiarity. She glanced from Vera to Natalia and back again. The sudden realization was like an electric current going through her. "Of course!" she whispered.

To double-check, she looked through the contents of her shoulder bag for the copy of the clipping of Irina and her chauffeur. They shared too many similar features for it to be a coincidence. She pulled out the faxed photograph and looked from Irina to Vera.

They were sisters! Nancy thought. Vera and Irina were sisters.

Now was the time to press her. Vera was exhausted, her guard was down. If the truth was going to come out, it would come now. Nancy had to seize the element of surprise.

She slipped up to Vera's chair, leaned down, and said in a whisper, "Mrs. Neverenko!"

Vera's dark eyes flew open.

"I have a picture here of Natalia's parents. Look at it, Mrs. Neverenko. Look at your sister, Irina!"

Chapter

Fifteen

VERA SHOT A frightened glance at the sleeping Natalia, then bolted into the hallway. Nancy quickly followed and put out a hand to stop Vera. The woman turned. "How did you know?"

"It isn't important," Nancy said quietly. "What matters is that I've learned who Natalia's father is. He's Victor Bykov, Irina's chauffeur. Now I need to know everything you know about him."

Vera looked through the open door where Natalia lay sleeping. In an agonized whisper, she asked, "Why must you do this?"

"Natalia has a right to know," Nancy said. "You've misled her from the beginning. And somehow, these secrets you're keeping are endangering her."

Vera's eyes filled with tears. "You don't understand!"

"Then explain it to me, and help keep your daughter safe."

Vera turned her head toward the room again, then pleaded, "Let us speak of this later. I don't want her to hear. Not this way."

Nancy was sorry for Vera, but she knew she had to be firm. "Let's go, then. I'll drive you home, and we can talk there."

For a moment the old fire flashed in Vera's eyes. Then she saw Hayden striding toward them, and the anger quickly turned to an anxious plea. "Not in front of Hayden, either. Please!"

There was nothing to be gained by forcing the truth from Vera in front of Hayden. But it was a tense ride back to the circus. Nancy was glad when she and her friends finally were seated in Vera's kitchen.

"Do you really think it is old secrets threatening my Natalia?" Vera asked, her hands trembling as she folded them on the table.

"I think it's possible there's someone besides you who doesn't want Natalia to find her father," Nancy said. "That may be what's behind these attacks."

"Then you should stop looking! Stop asking questions!" Vera said in a panicky voice.

"It's too late for that," Nancy said. "The only way we can protect Natalia now is to figure out

123

who is trying to keep her from learning her father's identity."

"If I tell you what I know, will you promise to keep my Natalia safe?" Vera demanded.

"I'll do my very best," Nancy said.

"All right." Vera took a deep breath. "Irina was my younger sister. She and Victor Bykov were childhood sweethearts."

Nancy was startled. "We thought he was American."

Vera shook her head. "Victor was Russian. He defected two years after marrying my sister. He became an American.

"Irina was beautiful and gifted." Vera's voice gained strength as she talked. "Victor was a homely man with big ears and big feet—and big dreams. Irina was only sixteen when they married."

"Sixteen!" Bess exclaimed. "That's so young!"

Vera nodded. "Victor was eighteen. He drove a truck, and he dreamed of freedom. Crazy dreams. Irina had dreams, too, but she was sensible. She worked hard at ballet. Soon she was a principal dancer. The better she became, the more Victor pressed her to defect to America. She refused. Victor became angry and said he would go without her. 'Go!' Irina told him. 'Perhaps I will see you there when I come to dance.'"

Vera was wadding a paper napkin in her hands.

"The stupid oaf left her! But it was hard for Irina. We thought she would go to prison for Victor's defection. And she certainly would have, had she not had such a rare talent."

"What happened?" asked Nancy.

"Just before Victor's defection, Irina had auditioned for the Bolshoi. There are very very few dancers who even get an audition," Vera added, pride creeping into her voice. "And they wanted Irina. She was accepted. But first she had to denounce her husband and divorce him."

"She did that?" Nancy asked, thinking of the photograph showing the laughter Victor and Irina shared.

"Yes. *She* suffered for what he had done," said Vera, with pain in her voice.

"Did Victor keep in touch?" Nancy asked.

"He tried," Vera said. "He wrote secret letters, under a false name, and sent them to friends who passed them on. Few letters came through in those years. But the ones she received were pleas for her forgiveness. Irina did not write back. It was too dangerous.

"Five years later, the Bolshoi visited America. Irina was the prima ballerina. When she arrived in New York, Victor was waiting at the airport with a limousine. He told those with the Bolshoi that he would be Irina's chauffeur as they toured the eastern cities. He led them to believe the United States was providing the service."

"That took courage," said Nancy, trying to get a feel for the kind of person Victor Bykov was. "Where'd he get the car?"

"It was his. When Victor first arrived in New York, a widow befriended him. She had a chauffeur business left to her by her husband. Her son was only eight, too young to run the business. So she hired Victor. Three years later, when the woman was dying, she asked Victor to raise her son as his own. He promised to do so. In return, she left the business to Victor."

"Did Irina recognize Victor?" Bess asked, and Nancy could see that she was hanging on to every word.

"Of course! Irina loved his boldness. In just a few days, he won her heart all over again.

"When the company moved on to more distant cities, Victor could not go," Vera continued. "But in three months, the company returned to the East for a final engagement in New York."

Her eyes darkened with pain. "If the troupe had flown back to Russia without coming east again, it would have spared Irina much shame. For beneath all of his success, Victor was still the stupid oaf he had been at eighteen."

Nancy wondered if that was a fair judgment of Natalia's father. "Perhaps he had changed."

"He wanted Irina to think so," said Vera bitterly. "When she told him she was pregnant, he pretended he was pleased. He urged her to defect. He told her they would be the happy American family."

Vera's mouth twisted. "The boy Victor called his son was twelve at the time. He was not pleased to hear of the coming baby, nor did he like Irina. But Victor convinced Irina it would all work out, and with a baby coming, Irina agreed. Somehow the Russian embassy learned of her intentions. The very next day, the KGB showed up at the rehearsal. They took Irina away and whisked her back to Russia—where she was imprisoned."

The tragic injustice of it twisted at Nancy's heart. "Someone must have turned her in. How many people knew her plans?"

"Only two. Victor and the boy. Irina thought the boy alerted the embassy."

"You visited her in prison?" asked Nancy.

"I was allowed to see her a few times. She longed for word from Victor. Thinking it might comfort her, I wrote to him four times. But no word came. He had deserted her again."

Vera added sugar to the cup of tea Bess had quietly made. But there was no way to sweeten the bitterness of her memories.

"Irina was released just before giving birth to Natalia. She had not had proper care. After the baby was born, she got pneumonia. She knew she was dying. She knew Piotr and I were to go to America with the circus. It was her wish that we take Natalia with us and see her safely into Victor's hands," said Vera in a tight, dry voice.

"You never adopted her, did you?" asked Nancy softly.

"I wanted to, but it was not what Irina wanted," said Vera, her voice trembling. "And Piotr felt a dying wish should be honored."

"Didn't the government object to your taking the child out of the country?" asked Nancy.

"They didn't know," said Vera. "When Irina died, we paid the doctor to say that she had died before giving birth. We hid Natalia for three months before leaving for America. We got her out with the circus, but we didn't know if we would be turned back for having a child without proper papers."

"How brave," Nancy said softly. She felt humbled by the strength and courage of such people. "What happened next?"

"People helped us, people who cared about freedom. They made it all right. They asked what name did we want on the papers for the baby. Piotr said we should put Bykov. That was how Irina would have wanted it."

Nancy watched the sadness on her face as she stared into her teacup. "I remember that afternoon matinee in New York. Piotr was a small man, and so agile! When they performed the human pyramid, he was the one who vaulted to the top.

"After the matinee, we quarreled bitterly,

Piotr and I. He was going to call Victor and turn Natalia over to that stupid oaf," she said harshly.

"A man who would desert his wife twice had no business with a helpless baby, I told him. Only when I threatened to run away with the child did Piotr compromise. He said he would test Victor. He sent Victor one of Irina's ballet slippers by courier and pinned a circus ticket to it. If Victor did not come to the performance, we would never try again to reach him. But if he came—" Vera paused and dabbed tears from her eyes. Tenderly she said, "Piotr wanted to give Victor a chance. I should not have vexed him—it ruined his concentration. I think he was scanning the crowd to see if Victor had come."

"Had he?" Nancy asked, spellbound.

"I never found out." Tears ran down Vera's face. "Piotr missed his last trick. He died instantly of a broken neck." She paused, her voice breaking. "I was out of my mind with grief. Natalia was all I had left. I took her and ran."

Gently Nancy pressed a tissue into Vera's hand.

"Even after I found a job with Marshall and he helped me gain asylum, I was fearful that Victor might track me down. So I changed my name."

Hating to press her, yet needing the answer, Nancy said quietly, "Vera, is there anyone who has anything to gain by keeping Natalia from hearing the things you've just told us?"

Slowly Vera's red-rimmed eyes met Nancy's. "I

am the only one. If she hears these things I've kept from her . . ."

"Trust her love," Nancy said, though the words seemed inadequate. Patting Vera's hand, she added, "I've got just a few more questions. Do you have any idea where Victor Bykov is now?"

Vera shook her head.

Nancy paused, thinking. Within the whole story, one slim possibility existed. The boy Victor had raised. The one who Irina thought had betrayed her. "Do you know the name of the boy Victor raised?" she asked.

Vera hesitated. Nancy reminded her, "As soon as she's well, Natalia will be completely vulnerable to whoever it is who wants her dead. Please, if you know the boy's name, tell me!"

"Dickie," Vera said finally. "Dickie Smith."

Nancy's pulse raced. Dickie! A nickname for Richard. Was it too big a leap?

Or could Bykov's adopted son be Richard Smith?

Chapter

Sixteen

R ICHARD SMITH is a pretty common name," said George, guessing Nancy's thought.

"It could be a coincidence," Nancy agreed. "But I'm betting it's not."

"What? What are you talking about?" asked Vera, looking alarmed.

Nancy turned back to her. "Do you know the man from Sunshine Enterprises? He's been here checking on the circus trucks. He was at the party last night," Nancy added, seeing Vera's puzzled frown. "Gray eyes, dark hair."

"Great tan," added Bess. "He was wearing a pink shirt."

"Oh, him. I remember seeing him, but no, I don't know him," said Vera.

"His name is Richard Smith," said Nancy. Realizing Vera might not be aware of it, she added, "Dickie is a nickname for Richard. And he would be the right age. I thought he was in his late twenties, but he could be thirty or thirty-one."

Vera looked so alarmed that Nancy hastened to calm her. "There might not be any connection. But if there is, I promise you, we'll find out."

"Go, then. Do what you need to do. Just don't let any harm come to Natalia!" Vera cried.

The girls left Vera's trailer and found a mechanic beneath one of the circus trucks. Nancy asked if Richard was around. The man said he was in Saint Petersburg at the company office and gave her directions.

As she and her friends sped toward Saint Petersburg, about fifty miles away, Nancy said, "I got the impression Richard worked in the business with his father."

"This is going to be a snap," Bess said. "We'll just walk in and ask to see Victor Bykov."

"We could. But if Richard is behind these attacks, we don't want to tip him off. We've got to get solid evidence against him," Nancy said. "First I'll see if the stem on his watch is missing. If it is, then we can be reasonably sure we've got our man. Then we'll lay a trap."

"And if it isn't?" asked George, who was riding in the front seat beside Nancy.

"I'll find out if he's Bykov's son. That shouldn't be hard—just look for a doorplate or letterhead with Victor's name on it. As for Richard, I'll tell him we're checking out Keiser's alibi and we need directions to World of Sound. If he's the wrong man, no harm done. But if he's the culprit, he'll think his attempts to set up Keiser are working, and maybe he'll get careless."

"But if it is Richard, how does he know who Natalia is? And why does he want to kill her?" asked Bess from the back.

"I don't know how or even *if* he knows. As for why, the only thing I see is that he had such strong feelings against Irina, he probably turned her in and foiled her plans to defect," said Nancy. Hands tensing on the wheel, she added, "There are a lot of unanswered questions."

The city limits gave way to sandy clay lowlands where gulls soared, searching for a meal.

"It's odd that Richard came to the circus parties. The account is already his, so it wasn't business," Nancy mused as she drove. "And he clearly wasn't close friends with any of the circus people. He always seemed a little out of place— unless I'm just trying to force pieces that really don't fit."

As they crossed a bridge, all three girls looked down. Below, sailboats and cabin cruisers dotted the rippling waters. On the shore they saw several beautiful, snowy white egrets.

About an hour later, Nancy nosed the car onto the exit ramp for Saint Petersburg. Soon they were in the city, where the streets were clogged with tourists driving campers and pulling boats.

Nancy was thankful for George's help as she watched for street signs, but it was Bess who spotted Sunshine Enterprises' headquarters. Nancy drove through the gates. There was a large lot to one side of the building. She parked, and Bess started to climb out.

"Wait a second." Nancy put a hand on her friend's arm. "You two better stay here. If Richard is our man and things get nasty, I'm going to need someone to get help."

"How are we going to know if you need help?" Bess asked.

Nancy smiled, a little nervous. "If I don't show up in ten minutes, get help."

The two girls agreed and got back into the car. Nancy continued across the lot and into the air-conditioned building.

There was a receptionist at the front desk. Nancy scanned the reception area. Just beyond the reception room she could see a corridor that split in two directions.

"May I help you?" the receptionist asked.

Nancy gave her name. "Is Richard Smith in?"

The woman picked up the phone. "Richard? There's a Miss Drew here to see you. Shall I send her in?"

Nancy waited as the woman listened, nodded, then hung up the phone. "He'll be right out."

So he wasn't going to invite her into his office, thought Nancy. Hiding her disappointment, she smiled and said, "Thanks."

As the young woman returned to her typing, Nancy edged closer to the desk. But the letterhead stationery in the typewriter had only a company logo, not the names of the officers. Hearing footsteps, Nancy stepped back just as Richard appeared in the corridor.

A smile lit his tanned face. "What a nice surprise! What brings you to Saint Petersburg?"

"Sleuthing," Nancy said, adding in a conspiratorial whisper, "Marshall Keiser says he missed the party because he was shopping for sound equipment at World of Sound."

"Oh, I see," Richard said. "And was he?"

"I don't know yet," Nancy replied, smiling. "I can't find the place. I thought maybe you'd give me directions."

Richard looked puzzled. "You found me, but you couldn't find World of Sound? The road into town goes right past it."

Big mistake! Nancy's mind raced for an alternate explanation. Smiling, she said, "I also found you because I was looking for you. I have something for you." She opened her shoulder bag and looked for her coin purse.

Richard smiled curiously as she snapped open the pocket-size purse. "Big gifts come in small packages, they say," he joked.

Nancy unwrapped the watch stem, then held it out to him. Watching him closely, she said, "It's not a gift, actually. It's a watch stem. Are you missing yours?"

"I don't think so," said Richard. His eyes moved to his watch, and he slid his finger beneath the expandable band. He stretched it out, turning the stem so Nancy could see it. "See? My watch doesn't have a stem."

The watchband settled against Richard's arm. A white line of skin as thin as a chalk mark outlined the band. That's not the same watch Richard was wearing yesterday! Nancy realized. The tan lines were wrong!

Goose bumps rose on her arm, but she flashed a smile, saying, "I thought maybe it caught in my sweater while we were dancing."

His eyes pierced hers. "You danced with quite a few guys. Maybe it belongs to one of them."

A shiver ran up Nancy's spine. Did he know what she was up to? It was impossible to tell.

The phone rang. The receptionist said, "Yes, one moment, please." She covered the mouthpiece and said to Richard, "It's Vic on the car phone. Do you want to take it here or in your office?"

Nancy kept her face expressionless, but her pulse was racing as fast as her mind. Vic! The final piece of evidence she needed!

"I don't have the figures in front of me," she heard Richard say. "Just a second while I get back to my office." To Nancy he said, "I'm afraid you'll have to excuse me."

"Of course," she murmured absently.

"By the way," he added, turning back, "if you'd like to do some shelling while you're in Florida, my invitation still stands."

Shelling? With this would-be killer?

Nancy forced a big smile. "That sounds like fun. How about tomorrow?"

Chapter

Seventeen

I'VE ALWAYS HAD good luck out on Siesta Key," Richard said. "How about if we meet on the same stretch of beach where the party was? There'll be a low tide about five in the morning. As I told you, that's the best time to get shells."

"Great," Nancy said enthusiastically.

"Will Bess and George be coming, too?"

Nancy's laugh was convincing even to her own ears. "There's no way they're going to get up before dawn!"

Richard lifted his hand in a wave. "All right. Just the two of us. I'll see you then."

Nancy returned his wave as she turned to go, but on the inside, she was boiling. He had destroyed Irina's life. He wasn't going to get away with destroying Natalia, too!

Nancy hurried out to the car and climbed in. "Well?" asked George.

"He's Victor's son, all right! He got a phone call while I was in there, and the receptionist referred to the caller as Vic."

Bess gasped. "Then you've found Natalia's father!"

Grimly Nancy said, "I've also found Natalia's would-be killer."

"So Richard was the attacker?" George asked.

"Can you prove it?" Bess asked, her eyes wide.

"I think so. He wasn't wearing the same watch he had on last night," Nancy explained. "The band wasn't as wide. It didn't quite meet the tan line on his wrist." Nancy raised a hand to stop Bess from interrupting. "Now, he could have just decided to wear a different watch today. But if that's the case, then why would he bother to deny that the stem I found could be his? I'll tell you why." Nancy answered her own question. "He knew he lost the stem during the struggle with me. He must have felt it catch on my sweater or noticed it afterward. He thought if he claimed it, it would give him away."

George asked, "But why would he want Natalia dead?"

Frowning, Nancy put the key in the ignition. "I don't know that yet. That's what's frustrating. But I've got a shelling date with him at daybreak tomorrow. I'll find out then."

"A shelling date?" Bess shrieked. "You can't go off with him alone!"

"I don't like it either, Nan," said George. "It's too dangerous."

"Not if I get lots of backup."

"Like who?" asked Bess.

"Marshall Keiser, for starters. Eduardo and Joseph. Hayden. And some clowns who were pretty heartsick over their joke turning sour," Nancy said. She snapped on her seat belt and eased out of the lot.

"They'd be useful in a fight," George agreed.

Nancy drove down the block and stopped near a small park where palm trees shaded dazzling orange and red hyacinths. An elderly couple in panama hats strolled past hand in hand. It gave her an idea.

"At five o'clock tomorrow morning, it will be low tide, and Richard's going to meet me on Siesta Key, the same place we had the party," Nancy began. "I'll get him to walk down where the undergrowth has been left untrimmed. That'll provide good cover for the guys to hide. I'm going to get him to talk if I can. Once he has, I'll signal the guys to move in."

"What's the signal?" asked George.

"I'll draw circles in the air with my flashlight," Nancy said.

"Okay, sounds good," George agreed, but Bess still looked worried.

A backup signal wouldn't hurt, thought Nancy,

keeping an eye on Sunshine Enterprises' parking lot half a block away. "I'll take a whistle, too. I'll give it a blast if I'm in trouble. Bess, you'll have to get it for me. And a hat, too. One that covers my face."

Bess nodded, and Nancy explained, "I'm going to spend the rest of the day keeping an eye on Richard. Natalia's all alone at the hospital, and he may make another attempt."

"What can I do to help?" George asked.

"I want you to go stay with her until Hayden returns. If I lose Richard, I'll call you immediately. Okay?"

George nodded as Bess asked, "What about me?"

"First, get me the hat and another rental car. Richard could easily spot this one. Then go to the circus and tell Keiser the plan. But don't tell him who we're setting up," she added quickly.

"Shouldn't he know?" George asked.

"Not yet. Remember what he said this morning about settling his own scores? I don't want him trying that with Richard."

"You're coming back to Sarasota tonight, aren't you?"

"Yes, but I'm going to make sure Richard's gone home for the night before I do," said Nancy, determined he wasn't going to get another chance at Natalia.

"Okay, then. Let's get going," said George.

Nancy climbed out of the car and waited on a

park bench. In twenty minutes, her friends were back in separate cars. Bess gave her a big straw hat, warned her to be careful, then climbed in with George and drove away, leaving Nancy a blue rental compact.

The day was long for Nancy. She moved the car several times, always keeping the exit of Sunshine Enterprises' parking lot in view. When Richard left at noon, she tailed him to a bayside restaurant, where he ate alone. After returning to Sunshine Enterprises, he didn't leave the building again until six o'clock.

Nancy followed at a safe distance to a lovely bayside home with clouds of lavender flowers and an immaculately tended lawn. She was tired and hungry by the time Richard turned out his lights, at ten. Still, she waited another half hour before picking up a sandwich to eat on the drive back to Sarasota.

Bess and George were waiting up for her. She filled them in on her day, then asked, "How's Natalia?"

"Doing fine," George said. "They're going to keep her one more day."

"She'll be safer there, until Richard's behind bars." Nancy sat down and untied her tennis shoes. "Did you set everything up with Keiser?" she asked Bess.

"I tried, but he was so busy all day, I ended up going through Eduardo," Bess admitted. "He gave me this whistle for you, and he said he'd take care of everything."

Nancy smiled tiredly, guessing Bess had been too intimidated by Keiser to approach him. It would be all right, though. She could count on Eduardo.

The next morning Nancy drove to the meeting place early. She'd put fresh batteries in her flashlight, and the whistle was around her neck, hidden by her jacket. Bess and George were coming later in the second car.

It was cold on the beach, and the rush of the ocean seemed overly loud in the quiet morning. Nervous, Nancy paced in the dark, waiting for Richard to arrive.

The sky was turning to shades of gray when his headlights lit up the parking lot. "Here goes," she muttered, taking a deep breath.

"Great morning for shelling," Richard called cheerily as he walked toward her. "Let's head south toward Rocky Point."

My choice, too, thought Nancy grimly. Her friends were waiting there. She glanced at him. Was that bulge in his jacket a gun? Cold all over, she stooped and picked up a shell.

They walked, few words passing between them. The powdery white sand narrowed to a path between green vegetation and the gulf waters. Nancy forced herself not to look toward the bushes where her friends presumably lay hidden. Rocky Point was just ahead. As they drew level with the rocks and the promenade, she stopped.

"Get a stone in your shoe?" Richard asked.

"No, Dickie, I just think it's time we had a little talk," she said, watching him closely.

He blinked and jerked his head in surprise. Softly, Nancy added, "You should have claimed the watch stem. When you didn't, you gave yourself away."

It was as if a veil dropped over his face. "What do you mean?" he said in a tight voice.

"I know that Victor Bykov is Natalia's father," Nancy said, tensed for action. "And that you're trying to kill her."

He stared at her, his expression unreadable. "Do go on," he said in that same tight voice.

Why was he reacting so oddly? Nancy thought nervously. "You didn't want her to find Victor. When I came to help her, you got worried and decided to kill to keep her and Victor apart, just as you came between Victor and Irina.

"Why is that, Richard?" Nancy kept her voice calm and steady, despite her racing pulse. "Was it hurt over the loss of your own mother? Or were you just a spoiled brat who had to be the center of Victor's universe?"

Sudden, raw anger burned in Richard's eyes. Through clenched teeth, he ground out, "No one could replace my mother. And I *don't* want a sister."

She had him going! Time to push a little harder. Nancy taunted, "Why is that? Still can't share, Dickie?"

"Victor will give everything to her! He doesn't even know she's alive, and he's been threatening to will everything he owns to Russian relatives. If he found out about her, I wouldn't get a dime."

"He must have his reasons," Nancy prodded. "Maybe he doesn't like you?"

Richard's voice shook. "He says I'm weak and self-centered. That I don't know what work is. But why should I have to get my hands greasy? Sunshine Enterprises was my father's company —my *real* father's! Victor's not going to cheat me out of it."

"You're the cheat," Nancy said, her disgust stronger than her fear. "You cheated Victor and Irina. You've cheated Victor and Natalia. For eighteen years, you've kept them apart. Victor's right about you. You *are* weak and self-centered!"

Richard glared at her. Then his hand went to his jacket pocket. Reflexes taking over, Nancy jerked back a step.

To her horror the flashlight slipped out of her hand. As she was bending to pick it up, Richard's foot slammed down on it. He grabbed her hair and jerked her upright, then jabbed the barrel of a gun into her side. "Scream, and I'll drop you right here. Start walking!" he growled.

Desperate, Nancy stomped down on Richard's foot with her heel. The element of surprise gave her a split second to jerk the whistle from inside her jacket and blow.

It didn't make a sound! Fear surged through her as Richard yanked it off her neck and flung it away.

The promenade jutted out over the water. Richard held Nancy roughly, forcing her step by step down the length of the walk. The drop was at least twelve feet, and waves crashed over jagged boulders. When they reached the edge, Richard jabbed her and said in a low, cruel voice, "Take your choice. Jump. Or get pushed!"

Chapter

Eighteen

D ON'T DO THIS, Richard. You haven't killed anyone yet," Nancy said in a tight voice.

Her heart leapt at the sound of feet pounding along the promenade behind her. She drove her elbow into Richard's stomach and whirled around.

But the dark specter thundering down the promenade was a dog. Hugo! He was coming straight at her, mouth gaping, teeth bared.

It was like a nightmare. Nancy saw him lunge and clenched her eyes shut, waiting for the pain. The dog hit so hard, he toppled both her and Richard. Richard's gun flew into the water. Nancy rolled free, bracing for the attack.

But the scream that rang out was Richard's! Then, above Hugo's angry snarls, Nancy heard running footsteps. Marshall Keiser, the Pomatto boys, the clowns, George, and Bess were racing down the promenade toward her.

Richard was cowering on the ground. Keiser called off the dog, then grabbed Richard by the front of his shirt. "I ought to finish you right here, Smith!" He drew back his fist.

"Stop!" Richard whimpered. "Stop!"

"Nancy, are you hurt?" cried George, helping her to her feet.

Nancy quickly reassured her friends, scarcely noticing the pain of scrapes and bruises. She was worried that Keiser might get carried away. "Tim, call Lieutenant Green," she said, and gave him the number. "Richard's ready to talk."

Tim dashed off to make the call. The rest of the clowns closed around Richard, hauling him off the promenade. Nancy followed close behind with Eduardo, Joseph, and her friends.

"I thought you were going to signal us," Bess said breathlessly.

"Richard knocked my flashlight away." Nancy's knees felt weak after her narrow escape. "Then the whistle wouldn't work."

"What do you mean, it didn't work? Hugo heard it just fine!" Eduardo beamed and patted the dog on the head.

"It was a *dog* whistle?" Nancy cried. "Why didn't anyone tell me?"

"Would you have trusted Katrina's dog?" Eduardo challenged.

148

"Probably not," Nancy admitted, her anger draining away. "Does Katrina know he's here?"

Eduardo flashed a sheepish grin. "Not exactly. I sort of borrowed him."

Nancy looked down at Hugo. He wagged his tail and poked his wet nose into her palm. She bent down and gave him a hug. "I never dreamed Katrina's dog would save me."

Eduardo beamed. "That's the circus for you. It's best at delivering the unexpected!"

Later that day Lieutenant Green called Nancy to tell her that Richard had confessed to everything. Green also filled in some missing details.

"It seems Richard Smith was a motorcycle racer when he was younger," Green said. "He could handle that Sphere of Death."

"How did he know Natalia was allergic to carpet cleaner?" Nancy wanted to know.

"He'd heard several people mention her asthma, so he knew about that. It so happens that Victor Bykov suffers from the same thing—and apparently, Victor once had a violent reaction to the same product," Green explained. "As for knowing to put it in a clown's white-sock, Richard heard the clowns planning their joke at the beach party. He also made sure Keiser looked guilty by planting the empty can in his office."

"Just like the postcard," Nancy said, thinking out loud. "He brought it into Keiser's office, then

149

planted it while I was calling the ambulance. And I fell for it!" She sounded rueful.

"Well, you had no reason to suspect him," Green pointed out.

"And then he canceled the call for the ambulance and sidelined me when I was trying to bring Natalia her inhaler. It makes sense now," Nancy said. "But there's one thing I can't figure out. How did he know who Natalia was in the first place?"

"Smith's very observant," Green began, and Nancy remembered something Richard had said about listening to people around him. "He saw Vera when the Russian Circus played in New York."

"When Piotr died in his fall?" Nancy said.

"Yes. When the accident happened, Victor ran backstage to check on his brother-in-law. Hearing he was dead, he started searching for Vera. Richard helped him look. In the confusion they got separated. Victor never saw Vera. But Richard did. He saw her run out into the street with a baby in her arms. Her resemblance to Irina was so striking, he knew immediately who she was."

"And he just let her go. So that's it!" Nancy said.

"After a couple of years, Victor moved his chauffeur business to Saint Petersburg, where he called it Sunshine Enterprises. Over the years it expanded into a very successful transport business. A few months ago, when Victor got the contract with the circus, Richard called at the grounds on business. He saw Vera and recognized her."

"One glance, and eighteen years later, he hadn't forgotten? That's incredible!" Nancy exclaimed. "Especially when he couldn't have been more than twelve or thirteen!"

Green agreed. "Of course, when he saw Natalia, Smith got very worried," he added.

"So then he made those attempts to kill her?"

"Only when you arrived and started searching for Victor. Then Smith decided to get rid of her and frame Keiser for her murder. Might have worked, too," Green added, "if it weren't for you, Nancy."

When her call with Phillip Green ended, Nancy and her friends drove to Victor Bykov's home. Richard had used his single phone call to call Victor, so Nancy knew he wasn't unprepared for news of Natalia. Still, she was very nervous as she rang the bell.

A tall, thin man with gray hair and hazel eyes opened the door.

"Mr. Bykov?" Nancy asked. At his nod she extended her hand. "I'm Nancy Drew. My friends and I would like to take you to your daughter."

Victor looked dazed. "I never knew I could

have such a day as this. How do you meet, for the first time, a daughter who is all grown up?" he asked.

"With open arms," Bess said softly.

Nancy glanced fondly at her friend. Bess always knew the right words at times like this.

Victor clutched Nancy's hand in his own. "Please. Take me to see my daughter."

"Right now?" George asked.

Tears of emotion glistened in Victor's eyes. "Eighteen years is much too long to wait."

The ride to the hospital, however, was not entirely happy. Victor spoke of Richard, and Nancy could see how difficult it was for him. His big hands trembled in his lap as they sped along.

"I could not have loved him more if he'd been my own flesh and blood. And now—he almost kills my daughter! What will happen to him?" he asked, as Nancy stopped for a light.

"Attempted murder is a serious charge. He's going to spend some time in jail," Nancy said.

Victor nodded sorrowfully. "He has to pay for what he has done. Life will not be so easy for Richard now." He was silent for a moment, and when Nancy glanced over at him she saw that his eyes were once again full of tears.

After a pause, Nancy asked him about Vera's letters. She was not surprised to learn that he had never received them.

"Richard always got the mail," he said. "He must have thrown all Vera's letters away."

As they talked on, Nancy could see that it hurt Victor terribly to learn that Irina had gone to prison for her attempted defection. He had learned of her death through the newspaper. But the article he read had made no mention of a surviving child.

"Then you never knew whether you had a child or not?" George asked.

"No. That's why I was so excited to receive her slipper and the ticket to the Russian Circus. I hoped at last to get some answers. But that went awry, too, when Piotr died and Vera fled. The other performers were scared," Victor explained. "No one would talk to me, for fear that the KGB would destroy them as they had destroyed Irina. Had I known Vera had a baby with her, though, I would have tried everything to find her."

When they arrived at the hospital, Nancy had butterflies in her stomach. They stayed with her all the way to Natalia's room.

At the door Victor gestured for the girls to go ahead of him. Nancy saw that his hands were trembling again.

Nancy opened the door. "Natalia?" she said quietly. "There's someone here to see you."

Seeing the serious expression on Nancy's face, Natalia slowly rose from her chair. "Is it—is it my father?"

Victor filled the doorway, his chin quivering with emotion as he gazed at his daughter. There were no words to bridge the gap of eighteen years.

Nancy's throat filled as Victor reached into his jacket pocket and pulled out one faded ballet slipper—the mate to the one Natalia had treasured all these years. Tears streamed down his face as he held it out to Natalia.

"Father!" Natalia ran into his open arms.

Soundlessly Nancy, George, and Bess slipped out into the hallway. Nancy took one look at Bess and passed her a tissue.

Bess dabbed her eyes and smiled. "I love happy endings, don't you?"

Nancy's next case:

An urgent message from Bess draws Nancy to beautiful Carmel, California. Fading movie star Joanna Burton has accused jeweler Marcia Cheung of replacing the diamonds in her necklace with fakes. But the case of the missing stones turns even more sinister when Ms. Burton ends up on the rocks—at the bottom of a cliff!

What led the actress to such a tragic final scene? Who pushed her over the edge? For Nancy, it's a murder mystery with more twists and turns than the Pacific Coast Highway, and she knows she's in a race against time. She must find the stolen diamonds before the killer strikes again—perhaps to put *her* on ice . . . in *DIAMOND DECEIT*, Case #83 in the Nancy Drew Files™.